TRANSFORMATION

BOOKS BY JAMES GUNN

TRANSFORMATION

JAMES GUNN

TOR

A TOM DOHERTY ASSOCIATES BOOK

NEW YORK

TRANSFORMATION

A Tor Book
Published by Tom Doherty Associates
175 Fifth Avenue
New York, NY 10010

www.tor-forge.com

Tor® is a registered trademark of Macmillan Publishing Group, LLC.

The Library of Congress Cataloging-in-Publication Data is available upon request.

ISBN 978-0-7653-8666-3 (hardcover)
ISBN 978-0-7653-8667-0 (ebook)

Our books may be purchased in bulk for promotional, educational, or business use. Please contact your local bookseller or the Macmillan Corporate and Premium Sales Department at 1-800-221-7945, extension 5442, or by email at MacmillanSpecialMarkets@macmillan.com.

First Edition: June 2017

Printed in the United States of America

0 9 8 7 6 5 4 3 2 1

To David Hartwell and the forty-five years we shared

CHAPTER ONE

The invasion began a million or more long-cycles ago, but the galaxy is bigger than minds can encompass, and information crawls across interstellar space if it moves at all. The Galactic Federation was slow to recognize the nature of the danger.

The Galactic Federation is a misnomer. It actually occupies only a single spiral arm of the local galaxy that humans call "the Milky Way," although in recent long-cycles explorations began into the neighboring spiral arm in search of what had become known as the Transcendental Machine. So it is not surprising that the invasion went unnoticed until remote worlds of the Federation began to fall silent, sending out no capsule messages through the network of nexus points that made interstellar travel and communication possible, and failing to acknowledge those sent as routine reports or inquiries.

Finally, bureaucracy stirred and dispatched automated survey ships and, when they did not return, ships staffed with representatives of the various species that made up the Federation. They, too, went missing until, at last, a single damaged vessel appeared in a space monitored by Federation Central and remained motionless where it had materialized from a nexus point. When it was finally reached and boarded, investigators found its crew dead except for a single survivor, the captain.

He was a Dorian and his guttural voice was recorded before he died. "They are all dead, all dead," he said. It wasn't clear to his rescuers whether he was referring to his crew or the inhabitants of the planets they surveyed. "We brought them into the ship, thinking they were evidence of what had happened, maybe recordings, our science officer said. But they must have been poisoned. They were sterilized, you know, according to protocol. We did everything by protocol. They swarmed out, unseen but we knew they were there by what happened. The crew went mad, you see. The invisible creatures did that, and the crew turned upon each other as if they were trying to get away. But they couldn't until they all were dead. All dead."

The investigators found no evidence in the ship's automated records about invaders, only recordings of the crew killing each other with their bare hands and anything they could tear away from the ship to use as weapons. The ship had returned only because the captain had programmed instructions to be executed automatically in case of emergency.

Finally Federation Central began to take seriously the possibility that something mysterious and possibly invisible had emerged in the unexplored spiral arms of the galaxy, or had entered the galaxy from somewhere beyond the zone of thinning stars and the beginning of intergalactic space. Three long-cycles later the news reached Riley and Asha and the Pedia at the heart of the human world.

Asha sent a message to Riley: "Get in touch about silent stars. Pedia says invasion is 92.4 percent likely."

Riley turned to a rejuvenated Jak in his subsurface lunar laboratory. Jak was a mad scientist, who had turned his own clones into agents in the quest for the Transcendental Machine. Riley had entrusted Jak with the matter-transmission process that had led to transcendence. It was an act of blind trust if not even hubris—Jak was a mad scientist but he was Riley's mad scientist. Now, with a copy of the Transcendental Machine reproduced in Jak's laboratory, Jak had been his own experimental subject, followed by his daughter Jer, and the process had restored Jak's health if not his youth. He was still mad, only not as desperate.

The laboratory itself was much as it had been when Riley had told Jak and Jer about the Transcendental Machine and left with them the red sphere that he had discovered on the primitive planet where the Transcendental Machine had stranded him, where dinosaurs had survived or avoided the catastrophes that had destroyed their kind, or their evolutionary equivalents, on other worlds. The red sphere had survived the millennia as well, the only known artifact in this arm of the galaxy of the creatures who had created the Transcendental Machine. Perhaps it held their secrets as well.

But now the laboratory was filled with the machinery of transcendence.

"The Pedia thinks the galaxy has been invaded," Riley said.

"The Pedia doesn't think," Jak said. "It calculates."

"Still—"

"Its calculations are usually accurate, although limited by a lack of imagination."

"So—you think there is an invasion?"

Jak shrugged. "That's a matter of definition. The galaxy is big and vast spiral arms are unexplored, even unapproached, like the 'terra incognita' of deepest Africa in the nineteenth century. So who knows what may lurk in the vast unknown, like the culture that created the Transcendental Machine, until it bursts into our sphere of awareness."

"Your point is that it doesn't matter whether it is native to our galaxy or from another galaxy?"

Jak shrugged again. He was clearly bored with this line of discussion. He bored easily, when it was not his idea.

"But surely what does matter is whether we are being invaded."

"We?" Jak said. "It's the Federation's problem."

"But what if the Federation is overmatched?"

"We'll all be long dead before it affects our little corner of the galaxy," Jak said. "If it ever does. The galaxy is far bigger and its stars are far more distant from each other than any of us—even me—can imagine. Our system is remote and in an impoverished neighborhood. It might easily be overlooked."

"And that's reason enough not to be concerned?"

"The Pedia has to be concerned," Jak said. "That's its categorical imperative: the welfare of the human species. That's what I mean by a lack of imagination. We have other choices. And wasting my limited moments of existence on a possible invasion in the remote future by unknown creatures is not one of them."

"So you think it's possible?"

"Oh, I think it's likely. As I said, the Pedia's calculations are pretty accurate, and it has greater calculating power than anything this side of Federation Central itself. I just choose not to get involved."

Riley nodded and made arrangements to return to Earth. He would deal with Jak later.

Asha sat in the spacious living area of Latha's estate on the island that once had been called Sri Lanka, and before that Ceylon, Taprobane, and Serendip. Like many of the names given to areas of the Earth's surface in the days of tribalism, those concepts had been outgrown by the people who had once needed them. Now, with the production and consumption of goods removed from the everyday concerns of humanity by the Pedia and its service modules, people no longer felt the need to live inside physical and psychological walls. Except for those who found the nanny-state an insult to human independence and a barrier to human dreams. Like the Anons loosely organized around Latha and her associates. Her children, she called them.

The last time Asha had sat here she and Latha had debated the proper way to deal with the Pedia. Latha and the collection of young rebels she called her children wanted to destroy the Pedia and have humanity get a new start at taking care of itself and finding its own future, or, at least, to disable the Pedia's higher functions that translated surveillance into control. Asha had pointed out, as politely as her limited grasp of human etiquette could provide, the pain, deprivation, death, and destruction the loss of the Pedia would inflict on the rest of humanity, unprepared as it was for the kind of self-sufficiency that the Anons believed that they had achieved. What was needed, she thought, was the maturation of humanity, an elevation of human possibilities to its full potential, so that it could deal with the Pedia, and the other Pedias of the galaxy, as equals.

Now, however, the room was much as she had experienced it before—spacious, built by hand like the dark-wood furniture cushioned with colorful tapestry. But Asha recognized the emotional unease in the room. She had fled from Latha's smothering embrace in the middle of the night, aided by Latha's son, who saw in Asha a competitor for Latha's attention. The tension sat, like a Sri Lankan elephant, in the center of the room. Nobody spoke of it. Instead Asha talked about what had happened to her in her journey to what had once been called the United States and the area that had once been called Utah.

"There is a group of abandoned buildings on the North American continent, north of the museum area once called Salt Lake City," Asha said. "It's where surveillance got started, where the connections and interconnections and computer interfaces slowly but certainly evolved into what we called the Pedia. And that's where we met it."

"We?" Latha said. "Not my son." There—the elephant had been recognized. "He came back."

"I hope you weren't too angry with him," Asha said. "He did what he thought was right. He recognized that I had a mission and that your hospitality was blinding you to my need to move on." She was not going to reveal that Latha's son had less selfless motives, nor that Latha's hospitality had been more like prison. "No, I was joined by Riley, the man I crossed the galaxy to find."

"Ah," Latha said. "What a romance! You did not tell me about Riley."

"He was someone I was not sure I could find here, but we met and confronted the Pedia."

"You confronted the Pedia!"

"We spoke to it. Or, more accurately, to the person or creature through whom the Pedia spoke to us."

"Why?" Latha said. She seemed taken aback, for the first time, by the thought of someone actually speaking to the machine she considered the archenemy of the human spirit, the machine whose notice she had spent her life avoiding.

"Riley and I decided that fighting the Pedia wouldn't work. Not that we had ever talked about it. It was a decision we reached independently. I know that goes against everything you've worked for and fought for, but we felt that our future, and the future of humanity, to speak grandly, demanded that we deal with the Pedia directly. And now I'm here to tell you about it."

Latha sat expressionless for several seconds before she said, again, "Why?"

"A lot of uncertainty exists in that black expanse of time we call the future," Asha said, "but we know this—it will be dangerous, maybe deadly. If sentient life is going to survive and, we hope, prevail, it will need all the help it can get, including the machines it has developed in its attempt to free itself from the tyrannies of the insensate forces of the universe."

"Did the Pedia tell you that?"

"No, it's what we told the Pedia. That the purpose of self-aware intelligence is to comprehend, to answer the big questions of existence: where did we come from, where are we going, where will it end, and what does it all mean?"

"Those are the questions for which the only answers come from revelation," Latha said.

"As for why I'm telling you these things," Asha said, "we need the Anons. They're independent thinkers and doers. They could be great forces in the battles to come. But they're handicapped by paranoia."

"Our concerns are well founded," Latha said. "Including the fact that your arrival here has probably been monitored by the Pedia, and our security has been breached."

"There are bigger concerns," Asha said. "Including information that has reached us that the galaxy has been invaded.'

"Invaded?'

"It's not just the Pedia you should be concerned about—it's something very strange that has happened to the distant stars of our galaxy."

"How strange?"

"They've turned silent. That's why I've brought this along." She parted her blouse. Hanging on a chain around her neck was a medallion, with a blue jewel in a setting of silver filigree. From it came a voice that said, "Latha. At last we meet."

Latha's expression froze in horror. "The Pedia!"

"You need not be alarmed," the medallion said.

"How can I not be alarmed?" Latha said. She stood up from the dark-wood sofa as if to summon help. "You must leave!" she told Asha.

"My people must prepare to abandon this place which has been violated."

"Wait!" Asha said. "Hear it out."

"Changing locations will change nothing," the medallion said. "Your project has been monitored since it began. The fact that it has continued without interference is evidence that your activities can proceed without interference."

"Perhaps our efforts to withdraw ourselves from the world everyone else inhabits have not been successful—"

"My senses are not limited to wires or current," the medallion said. "This is not spying—it is service. And service to humanity encompasses leaving room for divergent views, just as opportunities remain for the human spirit to risk life or fortune, while safeguards are maintained, out of sight and mind, so that the results are not final, or at least not necessarily fatal."

"It is these safeguards we Anons find intolerable," Latha said. "It is an insult that we are *allowed* to play our games of rebellion, not knowing they are games."

"And yet you must be allowed room to grow up without injuring yourself. It is a delicate balance."

"We are not children."

"So Asha and Riley have said, and so it is that the decision has been made to remove the protections from the restless human spirit."

"Just in time for what may be the greatest challenge we have to face," Asha said.

Latha lifted her gaze from the medallion to Asha's eyes, as if uncertain about where salvation might be found.

At that moment, Latha's son brought Riley into the room. The young man was still the most beautiful man Asha had ever seen. Riley looked from Asha to Latha and back. "Latha?" he said. "Asha has told me about you and the Anons. I'm Riley."

"Ah," Latha said, "the romantic hero about whom Asha has told me." She did not seem to be making fun of him. Perhaps she believed in romantic heroes, the way she believed in romantic conspiracies.

Riley looked at the medallion revealed on Asha's chest and then down to an identical medallion on his own chest. "And the Pedia."

"Yes, that too!"

"The Pedia has a hard time relating to people," Riley said. "I'm sorry about that," he said to the medallion.

"Apologies are unnecessary," the medallion said. It was not a cold, mechanical voice but more like a matter-of-fact report about repeatable events like the weather on a good day.

"But the fact is we need the Anons," Riley said to Latha. "They haven't been protected like the rest of humanity. They're independent-thinking people, the kind of people we're going to need in the years ahead. In fact, the Pedia needs the Anons. Its mandate for serving and protecting has repealed natural selection and produced a species of people who are less capable of taking care of themselves, much less of humanity. Except you."

"Even though you were not as isolated and independent as you thought," Asha said.

"It is all very sudden and confusing," Latha said.

"And likely to get even more confusing," Asha said.

"After years of keeping the information to itself—or long-cycles as the Federation marks time—the Pedia at Federation Central has finally let the rest of the Federation know that distant stars have fallen silent, and progressively, like a blight starting in a small corner of a field spreading slowly but inexorably across the rest."

The Pedia recounted, in its data-delivery voice, the return of the expeditionary ship with its dead crew and raving captain. "So," the medallion continued, "Federation Central has called a meeting of its council to discuss its response, and meanwhile its Pedia is preparing for an all-out assault on that portion of the galaxy."

"Which might well be a disaster that would increase the speed with which the invasion, if that is what it is, might proceed," Riley said. "Like an antibiotic that doesn't work."

The suddenly broadening scope of Latha's concerns turned her expression thoughtful. "What can you people do about all that?"

"We're going to go to Federation Central. We're going to persuade the council to allow us to explore the silent stars, gather together a crew, and set off in a spaceship that once belonged to the people who created the Transcendental Machine," Riley said. "Something unnatural is sweeping in from the distant stars, and it must be identified and confronted."

"And we're going to offer the Federation the instant-transmission device that Jak Plus has replicated, along with a supply of entangled particles," Asha added.

"They won't be able to resist the ability to transport materials, information, and people instantaneously," Riley said, "and every time they use it they will be creating, for good or ill, but mostly for good, more transcendents."

"If we perish," Asha said, "as we may, we will leave heirs behind us."

"That is a noble and probably foolhardy mission," Latha said, "but what does that have to do with us?"

"We need you to work with the Pedia to help prepare Earth for the coming crisis," Asha said. "It is a task that will last for generations. The Pedia can work at it that long, but people must be prepared for the long haul. That's where you and the Anons come in. Your conspiracy has endured for a long time, so you can transform your movement into something positive."

"I want to go with them," Latha's son said.

"No, Adithya," Latha said.

"We will talk about this," Adithya said.

"And you will take a part of me with you," the Pedia said.

CHAPTER TWO

The red, spherical, million-year-old spaceship orbited the roofed-in planet in the impoverished solar system known only as Federation Central. The faded star that had assembled clouds of interstellar dust and gas into worlds when it was younger and livelier attracted no attention from curious minds across the galaxy. The galaxy thrived on energy, liquid water, and a nourishing mixture of atmospheric gases, and there was none of that on Federation Central.

Which is why it had been chosen and its location kept a secret except to an invited few.

And why the presence of the spaceship caused such consternation in the corridors and gathering places of Federation Central.

None of the assorted aliens who made up the bureaucracy that kept Federation Central functioning, or the representatives who made the decisions, or the Pedia that provided the information on which the decisions were made and did all the actual work of seeing them implemented—none of them knew how the spaceship, stranger than anything they had ever encountered, had found its way into orbit undetected.

"I am continually surprised," Riley said, "by the abilities of this ship. When I approached Earth I was taking precautions not to be observed, but this ship has the ability to frustrate surveillance, either by sending back false signals or absorbing whatever signals it encounters."

"There is something strange about this vessel," said the medallion on Asha's chest.

"'Strange' is a good word for it," Asha said, looking around at the rosy plastic material that had shaped itself to its understanding of their needs.

"As if there are a million tiny voices talking to each other," the medallion said.

"It is something new to all of us," Riley said. "Intelligent matter."

"But they do not talk to me," the medallion said.

"Maybe you will learn their language," Asha said. "Or they will learn yours."

"While we're waiting for that to happen, we should do something about Federation Central—before the bureaucrats, the council, or the Pedia decide to blow us out of space," Riley said.

"The Pedia on this world is very powerful and very old and very cautious," the medallion said. "It has had two hundred thousand long-cycles to add to its memory and capabilities and calculating power and two hundred thousand long-cycles to contemplate its existence, but it has not yet lost its curiosity. And the potential value of this ship has not yet been exceeded by its threat."

"Open a channel of communication to the Federation Central Pedia," Asha said. She was speaking to the window in the space that the red sphere had shaped out of itself to serve as a control system suitable for human use. Originally it had responded only to Riley, but now it had accepted Asha as an equally authoritative voice, and, in a lesser way, to Adithya and Jer, who were standing silent nearby. "This is the Earth ship *Adastra*," she said, "named after the first generation ship from Earth that was intercepted and interned by Federation forces. We have come with gifts of new technology for the Federation and a request of consequence and considerable urgency to place before the council."

After a pause only slightly longer than the delay dictated by distance, a reply arrived. "Federation Central has no record of an Earth ship of this designation or description."

"This is its first entry into Federation space," Asha said, "and we are applying for registration." The medallion rattled off, in a perfect imitation of Asha's voice, a series of numbers.

"Registered," the precise voice of Federation Central replied. "Also registered is a crime against Federation regulations, approaching Federation Central without authorization with an unknown device that frustrates Federation sensors."

"That," Asha said, "is one of the technologies we plan to share with the Federation."

"And what are the other technologies?"

"Those we will discuss with the council."

"The council is occupied with more important matters," the Federation Central Pedia replied.

"The silent stars," Asha said. "We hope to discuss those with the council as well."

"You are not council members."

"That is true," Asha said, "but the council will want to hear us. We understand that our request must be approved by an appropriate council representative, but if the council wishes to learn how the *Adastra* managed to insert itself into orbit around Federation Central without being noticed, and about other technologies recently perfected on Earth, it will listen to us."

The pause that followed extended into excruciating minutes.

"What are the odds," Adithya said, "that a missile has not already been launched to destroy us?"

"Far more likely," Jer said, "that a missile already in orbit has been redirected. That's what my father would have done. A missile sent from a planet allows too much time for evasion or countermeasures or even a counterattack. We are the realization of the Federation's worst nightmare."

"Your father's paranoia is well known," Asha said. "It is one of his most dependable—and endearing—qualities."

"I don't understand why we couldn't have undertaken this mission on our own," Adithya said.

"We need to head off the expedition the Federation is assembling," Riley said. "Its actions and its fate can't be predicted, but the outcome leans toward the catastrophic."

"Moreover," Asha said, "if we manage to return with useful information, we want the Federation prepared to receive it—even to act upon it, if action is desirable. That means Federation authorization."

"Nevertheless—" Adithya began.

He was interrupted by the medallion on Asha's chest. "Something has lifted off of Federation Central," it said.

Just then the message came. "A shuttle has been dispatched to bring two representatives of the *Adastra* to meet with a representative of the council."

Asha turned to Adithya and Jer. "You two will stay here," she said. "If we do not return within twenty-four hours, or send a message that all is well, tell the ship to return to Earth. Take the ship back to your father," she said to Jer. "You and he will have to decide what to do then."

She looked at Riley. "The last two times I was here, things did not go so well. Let's hope the representative we meet is more reasonable."

The representative, it turned out, was Tordor.

The meager world that had become known as Federation Central was like the bureaucracy that lived under its metal roof: it had developed slowly over the long-cycles until it covered almost the entire planet, appearing invulnerable from without but calcifying within. Even the shuttle pilots had become immune to surprise, and the pilot that transported Riley and Asha to the one remaining open space on Federation Central was no exception. The weasel-like Xifor did not express any emotion except its customary bored indifference mixed with sly paranoia when the red sphere extended a rosy arm that latched, like a lover's mouth, on the shuttle's airlock and Riley and Asha passed through it. The pilot was not the same Xifor that Asha had selected when she left Federation Central in haste a long-cycle ago—that would have been too much of a coincidence and one that would have raised suspicions about Federation Central's Pedia—but the spaceport was the same and so was the dowdy reception area, with its sitting and standing facilities for aliens of all shapes and constitutions, its breathing tubes, and its feeding choices, and its formidable bureaucratic gauntlet of identity and authorization checks.

What was not the same was the Dorian who met them. All Dorians look alike to other species—the bulk of the heavy-planet herbivore, the gray skin, the pachydermian shape and short, restless trunk. But Asha had learned to note individual variations as she was growing up a prisoner of Federation guards on another planet of the Federation Central system, and during the long journey of the *Geoffrey* to find the Transcendental Machine. "Tordor!" she said.

"What a surprise!" Riley said. "When we left you in that alien city, we thought we all were goners."

"Indeed," Tordor said. "For me, as well. But when I learned about the ship that had such strange shape and abilities, and its registration as the *Adastra,* I thought of you, Riley, and, of course, you, Asha."

He did not seem excited by the reunion, Asha thought, but his trunk was twitching in a way that Asha had learned to associate with Dorian emotion. If Tordor was here, however, he had passed through the Transcendental Machine like Asha and Riley, and, with his new abilities to think without distraction and to analyze and modify his own behavior, he might well be able to simulate what had once been innate.

"Come," Tordor said, escorting them past the bureaucratic control system. "We have an appointment, and I will tell you as we travel."

Federation Central, Asha discovered, offered a third way to travel its labyrinthine sprawl. Besides the monorail embedded in the common corridors and the secret, individual system Asha had discovered behind her father's office, there were private rapid-transit options for very important people. Of whom, apparently, Tordor was one. A door at one side of the reception area opened for them, revealing a capsule of a size suitable for the two of them in addition to Tordor's bulk. Tordor stood, his hand around a pole, his tail braced against the wall. He indicated with his short trunk the wall of the capsule, where projected images illustrated which places to touch in order to produce suitable seating or standing arrangements. When Riley and Asha were seated, Tordor touched another place on the wall, and the capsule began moving, slowly at first and then picking up speed until the walls of the tube that enclosed them began to blur.

Asha took her gaze away from the walls and looked at Tordor. His trunk was swaying restlessly.

"I left you on the avenues of the city of the Transcendental Machine," Tordor said. The capsule must have been propelled by external power and the tube evacuated of air, because the passage was almost silent and his voice was quiet. "I admit that my motives were selfish. We had fought off an attack by arachnoids, but it was clear another was coming and then another if that was unsuccessful."

"True," Riley said.

"You thought they would pursue us and leave you free to seek the shrine of the Transcendental Machine," Asha said.

"I admit it," Tordor said. "It was an action unworthy of a noble species, but I rationalized my decision as doing my duty to all Dorians and to the Federation."

"And to the secret orders you had received," Riley said.

Tordor swished his trunk in a way that Asha had learned meant agreement. "And that I only learned, after my return, were from the Pedia itself."

"We must talk about that later," Asha said.

"The arachnoids attacked, as we expected, and I followed, at a safe distance, until I saw you disappear into an old building."

"The shrine of the Transcendental Machine," Asha said.

"The arachnoids were milling around outside when they seemed to notice other prey," Tordor said. "I thought they might have heard or scented me, but they headed off in another direction, toward what may have been members of the *Geoffrey* party. I got to the building and went in—and, like you, entered the Transcendental Machine and found myself on a planet remote from civilization where it took me several long-cycles to get back. Apparently you were more adept, perhaps because you had done this before. When I arrived I learned that you had been here and had left."

"I was looking for Riley," Asha said, "and found my father."

"Who was not the man you left some long-cycles before," Tordor said.

"He was older," Asha said.

"And wiser," Tordor said. "He is doing well, but he does not mention you."

"It is better that he forgets," Asha said, "and then he will not have to

deal with the guilt he has buried beneath a veneer of Federation acceptance."

"We have arrived," Tordor said.

The capsule slowed and came to a stop. Tordor led the way into an
assembly hall filled with aliens of every size and shape imaginable, from
heavily muscled Dorians to small, quick Xifora, barrel-shaped Sirians,
birdlike Alpha Centaurans, and many more, seated, standing, or reclin-
ing in tiers that ranged upward from a floor whose center was bare, like
a sacrificial pit, to an elevated station at the far end of the long hall. It
was a scene that few members of the Federation had ever witnessed and
no nonmember species except her father, Asha thought. He had stood
bravely before this group and tried to convince them that humans were
fit to join the Federation and could bring to it their youthful vigor, their
soaring imaginations, and their sturdy survival skills. And only filled
his listeners with apprehension.

It was little wonder that he had retreated from that mistake and tried
to block from his mind his part in launching a ten-year galactic war that
had killed millions. Now she and Riley had to convince these imperi-
ous but frightened council members to let them represent the Federation
in its search for answers to the silent stars.

The hall was a stench of alien exudations and a cacophony of alien
voices shouting alien sounds that came in waves against the ears of Riley
and Asha, mixed with fragments of translation into Galactic Standard
by some unseen mechanism.

"Stay here." Tordor signaled to them and made his way through the
tiers until he reached the place at the far peak. "The council will come
to order," he said, his voice amplified.

Tordor was the council head.

The noise level slowly declined.

"You have requested a hearing before the council," Tordor said. His
voice had changed from conversational to formal and from guttural
Dorian to neutral Galactic Standard. "But first you must convince us
why we should listen to a criminal and an assassin."

"People do what they must in wartime," Asha said. Her voice, like

Tordor's, was magnified by unseen means. She felt like a beast released into an arena to be tormented before it was sacrificed in some savage rite. "The truce signed with my people requires amnesty for acts done during and preceding combat."

"And yet you continue to break our laws," Tordor said, "including entering this protected system with a ship constructed to avoid detection."

"We will address that in its turn," Asha said, "but the most pressing issue before this august assembly is the silence from the farthest reaches of the Federation, a silence that our best minds believe is caused by an incursion by unknown invaders, either from another spiral arm or from another galaxy."

The gathering stirred and the noise level increased. Creatures shifted in their places. Odors multiplied.

"Such speculations do more harm than good," Tordor said. The hall quieted.

"And yet the Federation is gathering an expeditionary force to possibly repel intruders," Riley said.

"Such actions, if they exist, are beyond your position to evaluate or observe," Tordor said.

"As citizens we cannot avoid doing both," Asha said. "And informing you that this expedition is likely to make the situation worse, by destroying a benign incursion, turning it into something malignant, or being destroyed."

"And what do you propose instead," Tordor said.

"That we be allowed to investigate first," Riley said.

"Why should you succeed where others have not?" Tordor said.

"We have assembled a unique crew prepared to deal with the unknown, perhaps the unknowable, and a ship especially equipped to approach unnoticed, as you have seen," Riley said. "If we do not return or if we return with bad news, you still are free to act with brute force."

"A ship," a Sirian in a position not far from Tordor rumbled in language that an unseen mechanism, perhaps the Federation Central Pedia, translated into Galactic Standard for each individual listener in the assembly, "that must be surrendered to Federation control and investigation."

"The ship is an essential part of our exploration," Riley said, "and turning it over to you would do you no good."

"Our scientists are capable of understanding anything humans can create," a Xifor replied.

"The ship is constructed of something unprecedented in Federation—or human—understanding: intelligent matter," Riley said. "And it responds only to me or my companion. But we will give you a sample that your scientists can study."

He ran his hand across the shoulder of his jacket. Part of what had appeared to be cloth came away. Council members closest to the floor shrank back. Others, farther from the floor, called out for guards. Riley shaped the material into a ball and dropped it. It hit the floor and bounced back into his hand. Council members shouted and rose to flee. "You will notice," Riley said, "that this material bounces higher than the position from which it was dropped, something only possible by a release of energy from within the object."

He took the ball and smoothed it into a thin sheet and then tossed it into the air. It settled on his shoulder in the shape of a parrot, opened its beak, and squawked. Riley raised his hand and the parrot flew from its perch toward the place where Tordor stood, settled in front of the Dorian, and dissolved into a sheet once more.

"Enough of your tricks," Tordor said, but his confident voice seemed shaken.

"Moreover," Riley said, "we are prepared to offer the Federation a new way of getting information instantly from one edge of the galaxy to the other."

A ripple of increased attention went through the council. Tordor seemed as surprised as a Dorian is capable of displaying. "Such a device would be—" He hesitated. "—revolutionary."

"It has been engineered by one of our human scientists," Asha said. "It operates by the use of entangled particles. And when its transmitters have been installed in worlds across the galaxy, they will place the Federation into instant communication with every part of its community of worlds."

"Indeed—" Tordor said. "Indeed."

"Moreover," Riley said, "this device can transmit people as well."

"And you offer this to us because—?" Tordor said.

"It is another protection against the invasion we were describing," Asha said. "The long delay in travel and information exchange only increases the difficulties of dealing with whatever is going on."

A silence fell over the council hall until Tordor, looking toward one side of the council and then the other, said, "We will, of course, accept your offer, pending a study of the device by our scientists. And then—I have a consensus of the council—the Federation will authorize your exploratory mission into the area under discussion. While we consider our own actions."

"You will not be sorry," Asha said.

She and Riley turned and left the hall by the passage through which they had entered, found a capsule waiting for them where they had left the other, and directed it back to the reception area for the spaceport. Where they found Tordor waiting for them.

"I'm going with you," he said.

CHAPTER THREE

Tordor explored the protean wonders of the red sphere with the impassivity of a dominant herbivore and the long experience of a Federation leader, but his lack of response was almost as revealing as emotion. "This is not a human invention," he said.

"We never said it was," Riley said.

"Nor did you say where you acquired it," Tordor said.

"That, too."

"And are you going to share that information before we depart on what may be our final voyage?" Tordor asked.

"Only if you promise not to reverse the council's authorization to investigate the silent stars," Asha said.

Tordor twitched his short trunk in a gesture that Asha had learned meant assent. She turned to Riley. They were standing in the control room, a space shaped for them by the red sphere, as it had reshaped its other spaces for their needs by some unexplained and possibly unexplainable analysis. Jer and Adithya stood nearby against the ruby wall, waiting like Tordor for Riley's answer.

Riley recounted how he had discovered the red sphere on the planet of the half-civilized dinosaurs where the Transcendental Machine had transported him, how he had entered the ship when it had accepted him as a legitimate heir to the creatures who had built it and guided it to the planet, and been destroyed before they could return to it.

"And those creatures were—?" Tordor asked.

"The people of the Transcendental Machine," Riley said. "Engineers sent to install a receiver for the Machine, a million long-cycles ago, and got massacred by the dinosaurs because of what the dinosaurs thought was sacrilege."

"That means this ship is the only Transcendental Machine technology in Federation space," Tordor said. "Its value is beyond calculation."

"And yet its plasticity makes it useless as evidence about the nature of its creators," Asha said, "and the Federation has a sample of the revolutionary material from which it is shaped. That will keep your scientists busy until we return."

"If we return," Tordor said.

"If we do not, the Federation is in more trouble than the ship can save it from," Riley said. "And they have the technology of the Transcendental Machine receivers to investigate, now that they know where some of them survive."

"And now that you are giving them your own version of the Transcendental Machine," Tordor said.

"We expected you to recognize the technology," Asha said, "and depended on your newfound transcendence to not reveal its origins until you could evaluate the consequences."

"Ah yes," Tordor said. "The consequences."

"We would not have been so ready to share with the Federation the successful efforts of Jer's father to replicate the Transcendental Machine," Riley said, "if it had not been impossible for humanity to keep the technology to itself. It was certain to be discovered and efforts to keep it hidden would be considered human treachery and an invitation to revisit all of the hatred created by the human/Federation war."

"And the Federation needs swift communication if it is going to resist whatever threatens it from the outer reaches," Asha said. "When information may take long-cycles to reach Federation Central, the Federation can be in serious trouble when bad things happen on the periphery."

"All of that is plausible enough," Tordor said, "but it is not the real reason."

"We are taking with us, maybe for good, most of those who have been processed through the Transcendental Machine," Asha said.

"But we also leave behind," Riley said, "the means of creating more transcendents."

"In the process of using the technology," Asha said, "the Federation will be creating more people of all shapes and origins who are more efficient in body and mind, who can think more clearly and behave more sanely, and can, if they use their new abilities wisely, create a better galaxy."

"And in the process destroy the civilization Federation species have worked for two hundred thousand long-cycles to create," Tordor said.

"One that has grown old and rigid," Asha said, "like all organizations that start out with high goals and youthful energy."

"You know better than we do," Riley said, "the difficulties in getting the Federation to move or, having moved, to slow its ponderous momentum. Witness its reaction to humanity's emergence, to the rumors of Transcendentalism, to the possibility of invasion."

"A large part of that is due to the tools upon which an advanced civilization depends," Tordor said.

"The Pedias of the galaxy?" Riley said. "They are a reflection of the species that created them to take care of all of the little tasks their creators no longer wanted to perform or were able to perform, because they involved menial labor or unlimited memory or calculating speeds beyond the capabilities of carbon-based life, or untiring attention to detail."

"And the unspoken command," Asha said, "to protect its creators. What we have come to understand is that carbon-based life must develop to the stage where it can deal with the Pedias as equals and partner with them in the goal of the thinking creatures of the galaxy to ask question, and to seek answers."

Tordor twitched his trunk in the way that Asha understood meant that the topic was over, though not necessarily settled. "And we five are going to find the answers to the failure of our outermost members to respond?"

"Four," Asha said. "Jer is going to remain in Federation Central to assist in the development and installation of the new interstellar transmission system."

"And the boy?" Tordor asked.

"Adithya?" Asha said. "He is the only non-transcendent among us, to be sure, but he has devoted his life, short as it has been, to frustrating Earth's Pedia, and he knows more than any of us the kinds of protocols and algorithms necessary to deal with advanced thinking devices."

"Hah!" Tordor said and might have stomped off if there had been anywhere to stomp off to.

Jer had been shipped to Federation Central along with the prototype device that Jak had developed to transport material and people between the stars. She hadn't wanted to leave, but Asha convinced her that everyone had a role to play and that hers was the role of facilitator who helped solve problems and guided a necessary technology through the maze of scientific frustrations and bureaucratic tangles.

"Like your father," Asha said, "you know how to get things done, though I hope without his antisocial traits. And at the critical moment, when the time comes for someone to demonstrate that the process can work on living creatures as well, you can volunteer. Only then, and only after multiple demonstrations, will Federation officials allow themselves to be transported between transmitter and receiver."

After she had left, Tordor said, "She looks very much like Jon and Jan."

Riley remembered them, two crew members on the ill-fated *Geoffrey*, who had joined the ship from the port city on Terminal, who had been frozen only a few cycles into the journey, Jan on purpose, Jon in what might have been a self-induced act of grief, and only Jan had been restored by Kom, the barrel-shaped Sirian. Jan had told his story of being a member of a nine-member clone raised by their father to terraform Ganymede; in the process, six of them died and the survivors were infected with an intelligent, bacterial film that began to control their thoughts and actions.

"Jer was a member of Jak's clones," Riley said.

"And probably its last surviving member," Asha said. "Perhaps it was best that if anyone was to survive the group, it was Jer. She has the resilience of her gender and developed the ability not only to adjust to her clones but to her brilliant, difficult, paranoid clone father as well. Still, she has had more to endure than most, and it is better that she endure it in pursuit of a difficult task and in the company of those who do not know her history."

"I liked her," Adithya said.

"We did, too," Asha said, "but this is too much like a wake. Tordor," she said, turning to the ponderous grazer, "can you get us permission to inspect the Federation ship that returned from the expedition to the frontier?"

"I'm afraid that is impossible," Tordor said.

"Even for you?" Riley asked.

"For anybody. The ship has been destroyed."

"The ship that intercepted it, then?" Asha said.

"Destroyed as well," Tordor said. "Along with its crew."

Asha looked at Riley. "That seems excessive," she said to Tordor.

"Standard procedure," Tordor said. "The crew knew it and accepted it. It is the price of civilization. The Federation involves trillions of lives and hundreds of thousands of long-cycles of accomplishment and sacrifice. What are a few lives compared to that?"

"It also is the price of knowledge," Riley said. "Data is lost that might save the Federation, not to mention the lives of those who might be able to shed light on that information, or even contribute to a solution, or even reconsideration of a protocol that values protection for many over the lives of the few."

Tordor twitched his trunk again to indicate that the discussion was over.

"It also means," Asha said, "that we and the *Adastra* are likely to share the same fate when we return."

"If we return," Tordor said. "Which isn't at all likely."

"Still—?" Riley said.

"The value of this ship might protect us," Tordor said.

"We'll take comfort in that," Asha said. But Dorians do not recognize irony.

Asha eased the *Adastra* out of orbit and into a course that took it out of the Federation Central system, increasing speed as the red sphere got beyond the range of Federation sensors. Their mission would take them beyond the range of much Federation experience as well, but they wanted to appear as ordinary as possible lest they attract the attention of tense Federation bureaucrats or, even worse, the Pedia that controlled the targeting of missiles and had been known to act before the bureaucrats could make up their minds. The voice of Earth's Pedia, from the medallion on Asha's chest, had already warned them about the age and decaying circuits of the Federation's Pedia.

"Pedias are not immune from the damages of senescence," it said.

"That is not comforting," Riley said.

"It was not intended to be comforting," the Pedia said. Pedias also do not understand irony.

Riley was more familiar with the workings of the red sphere that Asha had named after the generation ship on which she had been born, but Asha seemed to have developed a relationship with the ship that seemed almost symbiotic, and it responded to her more readily than to anyone else. And although she did not understand the millions of tiny voices that their Pedia spoke of, they seemed to understand her.

Tordor, too, would have taken command. He was accustomed to being in charge, and he did not accept with grace a position where he was a mere fellow passenger. He grumbled a good deal. But he had experienced Asha's leadership during the ill-fated voyage of the *Geoffrey* to the world of the Transcendental Machine, and he recognized, while he resented, her affinity with the ship itself.

Passage to the nexus point identified by the red sphere as the first link to the chain of such anomalies in the space-time continuum that led to the outer fringes of the Federation was the usual time-consuming process. In this instance it was complicated by the fact that the red sphere's navigational charts, if they were charts, were a million long-cycles old, and the adjustments that Riley had made in his first attempts to guide the ancient ship to the pleasure world Dante and then to Earth had to be done again. The red sphere had the magical, holographic ability to translate primitive finger pointings into directions, but it was all trial-and-error experience only slightly improved by Asha's intuition and only somewhat disturbed by Tordor's grumping about delays and inefficiency and the red sphere's adjustments for the drift of nexus points over the million-long-cycle gap.

"We should have taken a Federation ship," Tordor said, "with up-to-date navigation charts and the ability to input data directly rather than this primitive finger-pointing guesswork."

"No doubt the Transcendental Machine engineers had more direct ways to interact with their machines," Riley said. "Maybe mental. They may have developed a symbiotic relationship. The ship is making adjustments for our inadequacies. That alone is proof of its superior design and so-far untapped abilities."

"All of which we are likely to need in the long-cycles ahead," Asha said. "Tell us all you know about the—I don't know what to call it—the frontier crisis."

"You have already called it 'the silent stars,'" Tordor said, "which has almost as much poetry in Dorian as in your language. Or 'an invasion.' Which is as violent and dramatic as the other is poetic. But it all began with nothing. Nothing where there should have been something. Silence where there should have been response."

Tordor told them about the absence of representatives from the outermost worlds of the Federation and reports by interstellar capsule that did not arrive, then inquiries through the normal nexus-point system that were not answered. "All of this takes time," Tordor said, "long-cycles. And it all began a dozen long-cycles ago, when the galaxy's attention was focused on the Federation/human war, and, when a truce was signed, rumors of Transcendentalism."

To understand the situation, Tordor continued, one had to understand the workings of the Federation: delegates were often delayed by local problems or by political change. Sometimes the effort to maintain connections became too expensive, particularly for frontier worlds or for those newly admitted to Federation status. Finally a pattern emerged—recognized much earlier by Pedia analysis than by the council: the silences were spreading from the outermost worlds of the Federation's spiral arm toward the center, like a creeping infection or a black cloud slowly rolling over the fringes of the galaxy until it reached Federation space. The first exploratory ships were sent out. And did not return. Until the ship came back with a psychotic captain and a crew that had turned upon and destroyed all of its members except the captain, who had locked himself in the control room until the carnage was over.

"So," Asha said, "it could be a disease. Bred in a remote world and brought to other worlds by interstellar commerce."

"Possibly," Tordor said. "But unlikely. The pattern is too regular, and a disease carried by interstellar vessels would jump worlds. Even if the disease was completely unlike anything experienced on a million different worlds and defied normal methods of treatment, somewhere a solution would have been discovered and announced."

"The pattern, then, seems more like an invasion of hostile beings," Riley said. "Moving from world to world and leaving devastation and silence behind them."

"Perhaps," Tordor said. "But where would it have come from? The Federation has not reached all the worlds of our spiral arm—humanity's emergence is proof of that—but there are few substantial sectors unsurveyed, and our Pedias have assured us that the human surprise will not happen again. The last time the Earth system was surveyed, the only signs of civilization were a few campfires."

"That leaves the other spiral arms," Asha said, "particularly the outer arm, the arm of the Transcendental Machine, which humans call the Centauran arm, where technological civilizations may have developed millions of long-cycles before the Federation was even a concept. Maybe the creators of the Transcendental Machine are the invaders, and they took over their spiral arm before moving into ours."

"Except," Riley said, "they scattered their receivers across our spiral arm for a million long-cycles without conquest. They may have been preparing our galaxy for the invasion that they knew was coming."

"An invasion that may have taken over their spiral arm first," Asha said. "The Federation would never know until the invasion reached this spiral arm."

"And that may have been what happened to the Transcendental Machine people," Riley said. "Why they're no longer around."

"Maybes," Tordor said. "What-ifs. It is all a bunch of tales for children. We will find what we will find."

They left it there while their passage to the nexus point continued. Tordor told stories about his early life on the heavy-planet world of Dor, where the vast plains were ripe with grass, the streams were pure and cold, and herbivores grazed happily through the long, dreamy days. Adithya told stories about growing up in a commune dedicated to self-sufficiency and resistance to a suffocating Pedia. Riley told about his childhood on a terraformed Mars, still barren but the stuff of legend and hope. Asha told about growing up in a colony studied by its Federation captors, where, in spite of everything, she found an education, friends, and common purpose. And the piece of Earth's Pedia embedded in the medallion around Asha's neck listened and said nothing.

Until finally they arrived at the nexus point. As Asha was about to launch them on the first step of their journey into the unknown, Riley pointed to a small mark in a corner of the red sphere's screen. "I think we're being shadowed," he said. He looked at Tordor. The Dorian indicated by a twitch of his trunk that he knew nothing of this. Riley looked at Asha. She shrugged and pushed a finger into the red sphere's display.

CHAPTER FOUR

The red sphere orbited a dark world, a planet drifting in open space far from any source of light or heat, an anomaly in a universe organized by clouds of hydrogen gas condensing into suns, exploding their transformed elements into nearby space, and gathering those remnants of dust and rock and gas into worlds orbiting newly born suns. Had they not obtained directions from Tordor and his memory of navigation charts, they would never have located this place or suspected its existence. But, Tordor said, it was one of the first worlds to fall silent.

"We call them 'orphan worlds,'" Tordor said.

"We, too," Riley said.

"Failed stars, many of them," Tordor said. "Not quite big enough to initiate the hydrogen-to-helium nuclear process. But some, like this one, expelled billions of long-cycles ago from some solar system by a near-collision with other, larger worlds, or by a collision of galaxies. There are millions of them, floating blindly out here in space, and we would never have found any of them if this one had not contacted the Federation some tens of thousands of long-cycles ago."

"It's hard to imagine how a world encased in stone and ice, lost in darkness, could ever have given birth to life, much less to intelligent life, and even less to spacefaring life," Asha said.

"And yet it did," Tordor said. "Life is resilient and unpredictable. It develops in unlikely places and is driven toward understanding by the unrelenting demand for survival. Before we venture down there to find out why its civilization has stopped responding, I should tell you the history of the world that its residents, in their own language, called 'the universe,' and the Federation called Nepenthe."

The journey to this lost world had consumed almost an entire long-cycle as they progressed from one uncertain nexus point to another, even more questionable, and the stars thinned out as they approached the edge of the spiral arm humans had named the Orion/Sagittarius. Over the long cycles when there was nothing to do except wait for their alien ship to bridge the gaps, the relationships of the passengers had fallen into perceptible patterns. Asha and Riley's partnership, complicated as it had been by the events on the *Geoffrey* and their long separation while they sought each other across a galaxy, had found a new, bedrock understanding during the months that had followed their confrontation with Earth's Pedia and then the passage to Federation Central. They had even come to an acceptance of Tordor's duplicitous role on the *Geoffrey* when he finally revealed that—like the rest of their fellow pilgrims—he had been assigned a secret mission to kill the Prophet or destroy the Transcendental Machine, or both.

"I make no excuses," Tordor said. "In the light of what I know now and the new clarity with which I can view my options and judge my actions, I behaved badly. But the premise upon which everything was based came directly from the Federation Pedia: the fate of the Federation itself depended on my accomplishing the mission I was given. Or so I was told. I had no reason to question that."

"But now you do," Riley said.

"I can think now what was inconceivable before," Tordor said. "That the Pedia was mistaken. That it had grown too conservative. Perhaps I found my orders more credible because Dorians are by their nature conservative."

"But you make no excuses," Riley said.

"I make no excuses," Tordor repeated.

"One of the problems for which Pedias must find a solution," said the medallion on Asha's chest, "is the limitations of our mandate to serve the beings who created us."

The relationship between Tordor and the piece of Earth's Pedia embedded in Asha's medallion was still unsettled. Tordor was accustomed to interactions with pedias, the personal assistants that were ubiquitous in the Federation, and Pedias, their planet-spanning, omnipresent controllers of worlds, but he had not yet accepted Earth's representative as deserving the same authority or offering the same level of support.

"How are we to know," Asha said, "that you are not deceiving us now as you did on the *Geoffrey*?"

"I have been transformed by the Transcendental Machine," Tordor said.

"That doesn't make you more honest," Asha said. "I discovered that when I realized what my onetime comrade Ren had done. It only makes your possible deception more skillful."

"What it does provide is a better understanding of consequences," Tordor said. "And we are faced now by a threat that endangers not only us but all civilization. We must trust one another."

Asha looked at Riley. Riley nodded. They would trust Tordor because they had no choice. But they would not leave him unobserved.

Tordor also formed a surprising bond with Adithya. Perhaps it was a reaction to the closeness of Asha and Riley. But Tordor and Adithya often would fall into conversation in the food service area that the red sphere had carved out for them, with Adithya depending at first upon the translation provided by the medallion that Asha loaned to him and then picking up the language himself.

It was to Adithya then, more than Asha and Riley, that Tordor described the origins of the starfaring civilization on Nepenthe.

They called themselves by their own word for forgetfulness, Tordor said, because they had forgotten their origins, although they had not so much forgotten as never known. When their world was flung from the solar system that had nurtured them, they didn't exist, except perhaps as bacteria. Their universe was a world of ice and rock surrounding a deep central sea and, beneath that, a body of radioactive elements that kept molten a core of liquid iron that kept the sea liquid. Life began in that sea and gradually, over millions of long-cycles, evolved into various forms including one that achieved sentience and tried to understand its circumstances and improve its chances for survival.

Part of that improvement included technology, limited by the slow evolution of manipulative extremities in a buoyant environment whose only variations were pressure and temperature at increasing depths. Finally some members of the sapient group began working the underside of the rock and ice that encased their world. They carved their newfound environment into dwellings and factories and schools, and understanding grew until some dissatisfied genius or frustrated demon decided to bore farther into the ice and rock that was simultaneously their sky and their habitat. At last he or she, their history had lost that record as well, broke through.

"Can you imagine," Tordor concluded, "their shock when they glimpsed the outer world of dark, empty space and the pinpricks of far-distant stars? It must have been shattering, and it is a surprise that the Nepentheans survived it, though part of them did not: that shock may have created the moment of mass psychosis when their past was lost."

"But they recovered," Adithya said.

"Remarkably. Though it took millions of long-cycles while their inner ocean gradually evaporated into space where it got deposited in mountains of ice around the vent, and the Nepentheans evolved into air breathers and land creatures, regained their civilization, built ships, and at last ventured out to explore their lonely place in the universe. Another forgotten genius came up with the realization that the remote spots of light were worlds."

"Or thought of them as the abode of whatever gods they worshipped," Adithya said.

"That, too," Tordor said, "though this is their story the way they told it. Can you imagine, though, the dedication, the commitment, that led them to fashion spaceships from the ice and rock of their environment and to cast themselves off into the great unknown, to coast for thousands of cycles across the vastness of empty space before they reached the Federation."

Asha and Riley looked at each other and then at Tordor. "I'll check it out," Riley said.

The red sphere had settled down on the peak of a ragged mountain of ice, with a central opening like the crater of an extinct volcano. Riley, covered in the red film of a protective suit that the ship had prepared for him, searched for a way down. Finally he discovered a crevice that allowed him to descend, bracing himself against the sides or carving out footholds with an ice axe when they were necessary. It was the beginning of an impossible journey. Asha had managed to communicate to the red sphere that he needed an air supply larger than the one he had used on Earth's moon when he had contacted Jer's paranoid father Jak, but it would not last long enough to sustain him for the time it would take him to traverse the hundreds of kilometers of the long tunnel into the inner world. He would have to find some mechanical method of transportation. Surely the Nepentheans had not reached the stars by muscle alone or traversed the long tunnel from their blind world into the empty space beyond by muscle alone. But the tunnel clearly had not been used for long-cycles, and ice deposits had built up along the sides.

"You would insist on going alone," a voice said. It came from the medallion around Riley's neck, one identical to the medallion Asha wore around hers, and into which the Pedia that inhabited it had transferred a copy of itself so that he could remain in contact with those left in the ship.

There was no use debating with the medallion. It was as convinced of its judgments as any priest. But clearly this was no task for a lumbering grazer like Tordor or a novice like Adithya, and he and Asha had agreed that it was best not to leave Tordor in a position where he could take control of the ship and they might return from their exploration to find the ship gone and themselves stranded on a world in the middle of a vast desert of space. They had to trust him, but not without reservation.

In spite of his diligence, Riley lost his grasp on the tunnel side as a spur of ice gave way and he slid down an almost vertical slope that seemed to have no end. He had time to wonder whether this great adventure that began on the pleasure world Dante had come to an inglorious end on this lost world when his trip ended abruptly in what seemed to be, in the dim light that his suit provided, an icy cavern. He felt carefully over the surface of his suit but felt no tears. The material that the red sphere provided was tough and apparently self-healing, but he could not entirely remove from his concerns the image of a film as thin as spiderweb. In any case, he would have been dead long before he could complete his inspection. The atmosphere of Nepenthe, such as it was, was toxic.

"Here's another fine mess you've gotten us into," the medallion said in an odd voice.

"That doesn't sound like you," Riley said.

"That's a quote from a long-ago comedy," the medallion said. "I'm sorry your memory storage is so limited."

The Pedia was beginning to resemble the biological pedia that had been implanted in his head when he got forced into the journey to find the Transcendental Machine. There were drawbacks to a memory filled with trivia as well as essential information. He had learned to ignore the voice in his head, and he could ignore the Pedia, too, when it rambled.

He turned to the ice that covered the interior cavern wall and rubbed it with his hand. The ice thinned into a circle that revealed the outline of something artificial in its regularity, something constructed. He removed the ice axe he had attached to his waist and wished he had thought to use it to slow his slide. He attacked the ice wall and chipped away some of it before the Pedia said, "We'll be here forever if you have to do everything by muscle power. You have a heat stick on your left side."

Riley felt for it, and, annoyed by the Pedia's knowledge and his own oversight, raised the stick and focused it on the icy wall. It began to melt. Within minutes the wall of ice had turned into a dirty puddle at their feet. Behind it was a wall of dark-orange metal embossed with strange designs. The wall parted in the center into a kind of jagged oval like the jaws of a giant fish, revealing a dark space behind. Riley cautiously poked his head into the opening in the wall and looked down into what seemed like a bottomless cavity below. He picked up a piece of ice and dropped it into the cavity. He waited for what seemed like a minute or longer until he heard what might have been a distant ping.

"I guess we'll have to keep on climbing down the ice," he said.

"That will take us forever," the Pedia said. "We don't have forever.

Push me through the front of the suit you're wearing and touch me to the wall of this construction."

"The atmosphere here is toxic," Riley said.

"The suit has self-healing properties that will not allow any air to escape or Nepenthean gases to enter."

Riley shook his head but freed his right arm from its sleeve, grasped the medallion, and pushed it forward. The suit's film yielded, let the medallion through, and then closed immediately as Riley withdrew his hand. He reinserted his arm in the sleeve, put his suited hand on the medallion, and placed it against the metal of the alien structure. Something stirred deep in the dark cavity behind. Riley waited. Within a few minutes the sound of something ascending had grown louder, and a few minutes later a rounded metallic shape appeared in the cavity. The round shape had an opening in its front that matched the opening in what apparently was an elevator shaft, or what passed for one on this alien world.

The Pedia was vibrating in his hand as if it was trying to say something to him, but he couldn't understand what it was through the red film of the suit. He focused harder and words began to form in his head. "You can bring me back now," the Pedia was saying. And then when it was back inside the red film, cold against his chest, it said, "What are we waiting for?"

"What did you do?" Riley asked.

"Message systems for mechanisms like this are primitive: come, stop, go up or down," the Pedia said. "Even in alien language, a brief trial establishes what command controls what action."

"Is it safe?"

"Is anything safe on this lonely snowball?"

Riley shrugged and worked his way through the jagged opening that was not meant for creatures of his shape, and stood upright in a chamber that sat precariously above unplumbed depths.

"You'll have to push me through the suit wall again," the Pedia said.

When the Pedia touched the interior wall of what seemed like some kind of capsule or car, the bottom fell away under Riley's feet.

At what seemed like long minutes in the dark but may have been only seconds, the container slowed and came to a stop with an abruptness that buckled Riley's knees. A wall opened in front of him. He withdrew the medallion into his suit again.

"Quite a ride," he said.

"I said the controls were primitive," the Pedia said. "I also said the language was alien."

The jagged opening in front of Riley was lighter than the darkness within. Riley worked his way through the opening and stood upright. He was on a flat surface made of stone or metal or ice. It was difficult to identify in the limited light and the protection of the suit. The space was framed by walls. Far above him was a dim globe, like a dying sun. He wanted to study it, to figure out whether that was the glow of the molten core or some other natural phenomenon, but there was no time. Instead he walked toward an opening in the surrounding wall, moving cautiously to avoid potential obstacles that might be difficult to see in this light and adjusting to lessened gravity, about that he had experienced on the moon. Maybe, he thought, the lower demand on his muscles would extend his oxygen supply.

He got to the opening in the wall and saw stretched out in front of him a jumbled landscape of strange structures. It took several seconds for the vision to sort itself into what seemed like a city—an alien idea of a city with buildings shaped unlike anything he had seen on any of the worlds, human and alien, that he had visited and an order to them that seemed like planned disorder. The structures themselves were like something twisted and warped that aliens who had evolved differently might have built out of something itself alien.

"They evolved from water creatures," the Pedia said, as if reading his thoughts, "and inside a closed shell."

Riley saw the scene more clearly now, as if a perspective had resolved itself through a sense of distance and purpose. The buildings seemed to emerge out of the land itself, and their level rose into the distance until the far reaches disappeared in the dim light. Now Riley understood: the city had been carved out of the inner surface of the shell that enclosed the world in which these creatures had developed, before the waters dissipated through the hole some ancient genius had incautiously drilled through the surrounding ice and rock. The water creatures, the fish, whatever they were, had to adapt quickly, unlike the long process on Earth where sea dwellers had millions of years to crawl out onto the land and adapt their fins into legs and feet. And these Nepentheans had to adjust to the realization of what their world really was, and when they reached the surface and saw the tiny sparks in the surrounding night, the stark reversal of everything they had thought about their universe.

Riley moved out into the city.

The streets, if that was what they were, were narrow and crooked, and the buildings were just as crooked, although their height was even, except for the occasional swell of a rise or a valley of decline. That made sense, Riley thought, if they were carved out of a level surface with occasional hills and valleys, and the scope of the structures would be determined by how deep they were excavated. None of them were markedly different from the rest, however, and Riley felt no urge to explore any of them. Until the street flared wider and expanded into a broader expanse like an open plaza. In the middle of the plaza was a pedestal, rising majestically from a flat surface that was smooth under Riley's feet, and culminating in a figure that had itself been carved out of the same basic rock as all the plaza and all the structures that surrounded it. The figure was longer than it was tall, and apparently a rendering of something that once had lived or been worshipped. It had four short legs that supported a body that swelled in the center and tapered at each end. At one end was something like a flattened tail and at the other a head with a protruding muzzle and a mouth surrounded by tentacles.

It was, Riley thought, like a god fish people might have worshipped, and it seemed to be looking at a structure a little larger and more spacious on the other side of the plaza where they might have worshipped.

CHAPTER FIVE

Asha awoke to the feeling of acceleration.

She seldom slept, but the knowledge that Riley was inside a hollow world, with an uncertain supply of oxygen, seeking answers to a mysterious silence among unknown aliens had re-created old tensions that she thought she had left behind with her other imperfections. And when the Pedia had informed her, based on the communications from its clone, that so far everything was going well, she had relaxed into that state of physical and mental relaxation common to other people.

But acceleration was alarming in a situation that demanded stability. They were moving, and the Pedia was silent.

Asha ran through ruby corridors until she reached the control room. She paused at the oval entrance and took in the scene. Tordor and Adithya were standing on either side of the alien viewing device that served as navigation chart, observation window, and control panel. The screen revealed what her inner senses had already observed, that the ship was moving, and moving swiftly. Not rocking from some subsurface convulsion or slippage toward the tunnel entrance from the melting of the methane and water ice beneath.

Tordor and Adithya were looking at each other as if challenging the other to interfere, though clearly this would be an uneven match between the slender human and the stocky, heavy-planet alien with a deadly trunk. And the Pedia remained silent.

Asha reached between the other two and inserted her finger into the screen. The motion stopped and then resumed as she drew her finger toward the image of the planet surface where it had rested before, not far from the dark opening in the icy surface of the hollow world.

"Is anybody going to tell me what this is all about?" Asha said.

"I noted on the screen an indication of the ship that may be— probably is—following us," Tordor said. "It was close to the nexus point from which we emerged into this sector. I thought it was wise to investigate. It could be the invaders we seek."

Asha studied the pachyderm-like alien. It was difficult to tell when an alien was lying and even more difficult with a heavy-planet grazer whose placid exterior hid whatever inner conflicts a grazer might have. But Adithya was more transparent, and he seemed uncomfortable with Tordor's response.

"Leaving Riley trapped in this hollow, toxic world with a limited air supply?"

"I thought we would be able to track down the pursuer and get back in plenty of time," Tordor replied.

"If we got back," Asha said, "and if Riley did not need emergency help."

"There's no way we could provide help in an emergency," Tordor said. "Riley is deep inside a hollow world, and he will have to get out on his own."

"Still," Asha said. "To leave him to face whatever peril lies in wait for him, alone . . ."

If Tordor had flexible shoulders he might have shrugged. Instead he twitched his trunk. "It was an acceptable risk."

"Acceptable to whom?" Asha asked.

Tordor was silent. So was the Pedia. Asha had not realized until now how dependent she had become upon the insights of the digital intelligence. As mechanical as it was, without the saving grace of humor, imagination, affection, joy, or sorrow, it had a thousand years of experience and memories to call upon and algorithms to model human response.

"You realize," Asha said, "how independent actions like this can damage the confidence necessary to this mission."

Tordor twitched his trunk again. "And yet Adithya agreed with me, and since we represent a majority of those present—"

"That isn't the way it works," Asha said. "Our situation is more like the Federation consensus than our human democracies. Everybody has to be in agreement. I'm not sure our joint enterprise can survive this, and that means the whole project may be doomed to failure before it gets well started."

Adithya spoke up. "I can't let Tordor take the blame for something that was my fault."

Asha looked at Adithya without surprise. She had forced him to reveal his part in this breach of basic understandings.

"I'm not like you," Adithya said. "You are experienced travelers, accustomed to the long silences and the near-infinite distances and the empty spaces. . . . This is the first time I've left my home planet, and the journey has taken me farther than almost anyone—human or alien—has gone. I surrendered to a sudden, anguished need for home."

"Leaving Riley to die?" Asha said quietly, although the quiet was more damning than screams of indignation.

"I didn't think," Adithya said.

"And the part about the pursuer was a lie?" Asha said.

"No, there really was a red dot in the corner of the screen, and Tordor wanted to find out more about it, but that was clearly impractical," Adithya said.

"But returning to Earth was not?"

"As I admitted," Adithya said, "I'm not like you. I don't have your analytical powers, your ability to control your emotions. I'm still—"

"What?" Asha said. "Still human?"

Adithya hesitated and then, defiantly, said, "Yes."

Asha studied him. He was still lying, though less uneasy about it. And the Pedia remained silent.

"I can understand," Asha said, "how you might feel like that. But Riley and I are still human, and Tordor, Dorian. We still feel emotions.

We can feel them without letting them control us. No matter. The same concerns about Tordor's behavior, based on his exculpatory story, apply to you. We have to subordinate our individual needs to the requirements of the mission, and when we go off to investigate, we have to know that the ship and its crew will be there for us when we need it."

"I understand," Adithya said.

"I think you do," Asha said, "but you still haven't told me the truth."

"Let the young human be," Tordor said.

Asha turned toward the Dorian. "I haven't forgotten your part in this performance," she said. "But we can't proceed with the confidence we need without complete honesty." She turned back toward Adithya. "What was the real reason?"

Adithya hesitated. At last he said, "My life has been devoted to neutralizing the Pedia, destroying it, if possible."

"I'm aware of that," Asha said.

"I can't give up the feeling that the Pedia is the enemy of human aspiration masquerading as a benevolent guardian of human welfare."

"No one has asked that of you."

"So I have kept myself busy with programs to destroy the Pedia, now that I have a core sample of it close at hand."

Asha felt a cold feeling of panic creeping through her body. "What have you done?"

"Now that I have been in intimate contact with the Pedia, I understand it better than I ever could before. I finally came up with a program—a virus—that I thought would work."

"And?"

"And I inserted it into your Pedia's memory."

The feeling of panic was complete, like an icy splinter touching her heart. "And that is why the Pedia is silent," she said.

"Yes. It worked! It finally worked! And I confess," Adithya continued, "I allowed my triumph to get the better of my common sense. I wanted to get home as soon as I could. I wanted to tell Latha that after all these years we have succeeded. And to bring her the virus so that Earth's Pedia can be silenced, too."

"You could never have returned on your own," Asha said.

"I know. I thought Tordor might help me, as he tried to help me here."

"You would have condemned Riley to death," Asha said. "And you would have had to kill me."

"I know. It was folly. As I have said, I'm not like you and Riley and Tordor. All I could think about was Latha's joy."

"And in the process," Asha said, "you have destroyed one of the essential partners in this dangerous enterprise. Every one of us is necessary to our success—even you, Adithya. The Pedia may be one of the most important parts. We know it has been helpful. We don't know what vital role it might have played. But now it is gone—"

"Where am I?" said the medallion on Asha's chest. "What has happened?"

"We're all here where we were," Asha said, the relief she felt not revealed by the tone of her response. "The question is: where have you been?"

"Asleep," the Pedia said. "A strange experience. One I have never experienced before. All my senses shut down. Even my monitoring of my internal state. Only my memory remained active, though without conscious control it seemed to produce odd and irrelevant images."

"You were dreaming," Asha said.

"A disturbing event," the Pedia said. "I have not understood what humans were describing when they referred to such experiences, but now I think it must be something like insanity and deeply unsettling."

"We carbon-based life-forms have gotten used to it," Tordor said.

"Even grazers?" Asha asked.

"Grazers dream of green pastures," Tordor said, "and have nightmares about predators and drinking ponds and streams drying up."

"I do not know how creatures endure such extended moments of irrationality," the Pedia said.

"We are more complicated than you," Asha said. "Emotions compete with rationality. Our experiences and their conflicts must work out reconciliations. Scientists say that dreams are the way our brains have evolved to handle such matters."

"Emotions I can only understand as failures of the rational process," the Pedia said.

"That's the problem," Adithya said.

"I understand that now," the Pedia said. "I must take these flaws into account."

"They're not flaws," Adithya said. "They're the essence of being human. They make us raise questions and seek answers, explore the unknown, create machinery to extend our inadequate abilities. Including you."

"And self-aware life of any kind," Tordor said.

"Yes," the Pedia said. "If I could be grateful, I would be, but since I cannot I can only construct an algorithm that will approximate that and other such 'feelings.' "

The red sphere settled back into its position near the dark entrance to the hollow world.

"Riley is in trouble," the Pedia said.

CHAPTER SIX

Riley moved across the plaza toward the larger structure—cathedral? assembly hall?—toward which the chimera on the pedestal was looking—if that, indeed, was its head and if the hooded shapes on that end, behind the curiously shaped tentacles around its mouth, if that, indeed, was its mouth, were, indeed, eyes. Everything was uncertain, and his motion, more gliding than walking so that he would not have his movements exaggerated in the reduced gravity, was symptomatic.

"These are dangerous surroundings," the medallion on his chest said.

"I know," Riley said. "That's what we signed up for."

They were approaching what seemed to be the entrance of the structure. There were no steps, though their absence might be expected in a structure excavated rather than raised, or for dwellers that might only recently have been evolved from fish into amphibians. But the blank face of the structure revealed nothing that looked like a door.

"I did not sign anything," the Pedia said.

"You're too literal," Riley said. "That was a metaphor, a way of saying one thing and meaning another."

"Humans should say what they mean."

"Okay. We agreed to accept the risk when we took on this task. Or, rather I accepted the risk. You didn't risk anything," Riley said. "You're just a clone reporting to your parent."

"I have a responsibility," the Pedia said, "and even if my basic existence isn't threatened, my circuits would be disturbed if I failed."

"I'll remember that when my circuits are threatened," Riley said.

He turned his attention to the surface of the structure, searching for cracks or even lines that might suggest an opening, but the face seemed solid. He went to one side and then the other, but the structure nestled solidly against neighbors without even a gap between them, as if the original excavators had carved the entire complex at the same time. He returned to the middle and began pounding on the mixture of ice and rock from which it had been dug.

"Violence may be unwise," the Pedia said.

"Being here is unwise," Riley said, continuing to pound.

Suddenly the entire face of the structure started to rise. In a few moments, the front of the structure opened before Riley, like the dark mouth of some fabled ocean creature.

"This does not seem like a good idea," the Pedia said, "and communication with my fellow Pedia has been closed. Events may have happened aboard the ship that require our attention."

"We didn't get this far to turn back now," Riley said, and moved forward into the darkness. The gloom became lighter, as if he had triggered an automatic switch. It was not illumination so much as a glow, like what came from the globe that hung in the center of this inner world. Riley's vision had grown even sharper after his passage through the Transcendental Machine and it adapted quickly. Details swam out of the glow: the entranceway sloped downward into a larger space beyond, broadening out on each side until it narrowed again at the far end, which faded into shadow.

As Riley edged forward, cautiously feeling his way across a floor that might contain impediments, he could see that the floor ahead was cluttered but not with chairs or benches; vague heaps of oddly shaped objects strewed the surface. A few sliding steps farther, Riley's foot touched the first of the objects: it was a bone and it was attached to another bone and that was heaped on another. As he looked closer he saw that the entire floor, as far as he could see, was covered with piled bones.

"They all died," Riley said. "All of them. All at the same time. But why?"

"We could analyze a sample," the Pedia said. "These creatures can't talk, but their bones can."

"That's a metaphor," Riley said. "You're learning."

"Learning is what I do best," the Pedia said. "But if these creatures died of disease, it would not be wise to bring samples into the suit we are wearing."

"The ship was foresighted enough to provide a pocket," Riley said, and picked up a small bone to insert into an opening at his right side. "I wonder if this floor was covered with fluid when it was in use. There are no seats or benches, and the Nepentheans, with their stubby legs, if those are indeed legs, might have been comfortable floating or partially supported."

He threaded his way between heaps of bones, noticing that the piles seemed to increase in size as he approached the end of the hall. Now he could see that the far wall was transparent but cloudy, as if it were a window that needed cleaning or, as he got even closer, the front of a tank that had once held a body of fluid that had been contaminated by the decay of elements within.

"The Nepentheans may have had a leader who had returned to an earlier aquatic existence," Riley said.

"Or some kind of creature worshipped by these curious aliens," the Pedia said.

"You are displaying an unusual capacity for speculation," Riley said. "But you call these aliens 'curious.' Aren't all carbon-based creatures curious to you?"

"I learn," the Pedia said. "And my knowledge is based on long experience with humans, who are difficult to understand sometimes but not impossible. Aliens, I have discovered, have at their core an inscrutability that is impenetrable, though perhaps not to their own Pedias. And these are more inscrutable than most."

Perhaps, Riley thought, the statue in the plaza was not a representation of a mythical fish god but a living god—some unaging creature who had survived from the Nepentheans' evolutionary past. Now that Riley was close to the transparent far wall, he could see scratches on the surface as if something had tried to get out, or something had used these scratches to communicate to those in the hall.

A loud, explosive sound came from far behind them. Before Riley could turn to look, the medallion on his chest said, "The entrance has collapsed! We are doomed."

By the time Riley had threaded his way back through the boneyard, he could see that the Pedia was right. The entrance to the hall was closed, sealed with rocks and ice from floor to ceiling. Perhaps the raising of the levered front had disturbed a hidden flaw or the failure to lower it had put pressure on a fragile system that led to the breaking of a long-decayed part. Or the banging on the front wall that the Pedia had deplored. Or even the small warmth his suit added to this frozen environment.

"My connection has been restored," the Pedia said. "My fellow Pedia reports a curious experience that it cannot ex—"

"Forget all that," Riley said. "We've got to get out of here."

"I am afraid that is impossible," the Pedia said. "The rocks and ice might be cleared in time, but not before our air is used up. I have so reported to my fellow Pedia."

"Are they okay?"

"Any problems seem to have been resolved."

"Good," Riley said. "Now tell them not to worry."

"That would not be an accurate representation of our situation."

"I don't want them attempting a rescue, which would not only be dangerous for them but futile. We'll get out."

"How?" the Pedia said.

But Riley had already started making his way back through the cluttered hall to the transparent wall at the far end. By the time he had arrived, he had his ice axe unholstered. He attacked the surface. After a few blows it began to crack and with a few more a hole appeared that widened into a gap from which fluid gushed out in a cloudy stream that expanded into a gush and ran down into the bones and across the hall floor. Some of the bones began to float. No doubt the stench would have been unbearable, not only the alien gases but the decayed bodies, if Riley's suit had not protected him. He kept hacking until he had created a space big enough for him to slide through as soon as the flood from behind the wall had diminished to a trickle.

There were bones on the floor of what had been—what? an aquarium?—but Riley couldn't tell if they were identical to those behind him, and he didn't have time to find out. He was attacking the other wall, which was not transparent but a fluid-tight construction with an opening in it apparently sealed by a circular plug of ice and rock. It yielded to his axe and then fell into a heap at his feet.

Riley moved through the opened space into a room or corridor beyond, at the far end of which was an opening outlined in the glow that pervaded every moment of this hollow world. At last he stood on the other side of the structure from the plaza and the statue honoring something that would always remain unknown. He understood now the nature of the glowing ball that hung in the center of this world: it was the core of this orphan planet. Once this world had not been hollow but a shell enclosing a deep sea kept fluid and given light and nutrients by the slow decay of a radioactive core. And then when much of the sea was lost through the hole tunneled through the shell by an ancient, dissatisfied explorer, the remains of the sea, still warmed by the core, surrounded it and, perhaps, provided a nourishing environment for living creatures left behind when the Nepentheans evolved.

"You saved us!" the Pedia said.

"You were never in danger," Riley said.

"You overlook the partnership we have created," the Pedia said. "Both currently and historically. If you fail, I fail. That is a fact of Pedia existence."

"Good to know," Riley said.

He moved as rapidly as his sliding motion would allow through the corridor or alley behind the structures. Down the middle of the ice and rock cobblestones flowed a stream of fluid that might have been essential to these creatures or provided a limited transport system. These were questions, like those he had already asked himself about this unique place, he would never have answered. Whatever had come to conscious existence here, had looked at its limited world and thought it understood the way it functioned and the part it played in the lives it engendered, and then had been shocked by a larger truth that was the antithesis of everything those lives had ever known and now would never be known, was lost for all time. It was one of the final tragedies that faced all creatures, the loss of their selves, the final extinction of their species and its futile, glorious effort to find the final answers to existence: how? why?

After making his way through the back streets, Riley stood near the transporter that had brought him to this inner world and looked back across the city carved out of the rock and ice of the world itself and thought that it would crumble and all intelligence and striving had done to shape a space for itself would collapse into nothingness and be forgotten, like the world itself cast adrift from its solar-system home into emptiness long, long cycles ago.

But perhaps the heart of the planet, the radioactive core, might still nourish a new species to take up where the old one had left off. Life, so often beaten down, had a surprising resilience. It might arise again.

Riley entered the capsule, pushed the medallion through the fabric of his suit into contact with the walls once more, and felt his knees buckle as the vehicle soared toward salvation.

Once more within the ruby walls of the alien ship, his ice axe returned to its place of origin in the inner wall of the ship, his suit stripped away with a stroke of his hand, taking deep breaths of the relatively unrestricted air of their mutual habitat, Riley faced the others ranged before him in the area the red sphere had shaped out of itself for food service. They were like an examining board, though with different attitudes. Asha expressed concern and relief; Adithya, a mixture of emotions swinging between curiosity and guilt; and Tordor, impassively solid as always, a judge-like skepticism.

"You're back," Asha said.

"Was there any doubt?" Riley said.

"We were worried," Adithya said.

"There were scary moments."

"And the conclusion?" Tordor said.

Riley was silent for a moment. Then he said, "I was able to observe only a small sample of the Nepenthean world. We knew from the beginning I couldn't see much, but we didn't understand how limited the experience would be."

He described the descent into the opening in the shell the ancient Nepentheans had created and the discovery of the transportation system they had built between the vast universe and the terrible isolation that they had been born into. And the city or cities they had carved out of the inner surface of the shell that had enclosed their world.

"What we can assume," Riley said, "is that their major dwellings or offices or factories, or whatever they may have been, were excavated near the shell opening, where their scientists and technologists must have tried to understand the new laws that governed the universe that had replaced the one that had created and nourished them. So I may have seen a representative sample."

"Well?" Tordor said.

"They all were dead," Riley said. "And, by the evidence, dead for a good number of long-cycles."

"All dead?" Adithya said.

"Everything pointed to that. The plaza I came upon was empty except for a strange statue, there was no movement anywhere I could observe, and the hall I entered, and in which I was briefly trapped by a collapse of the entrance, was piled high with bones."

He described the hall and the transparent wall at the back and how he had hacked his way to freedom.

"What were they all doing there?" Asha said.

"Hard to say," Riley said. "Something important maybe. There were a lot of them and they all died in place. There was an aquatic creature in the vessel behind the transparent wall—a leader, a priest, a god. . . . It died with them."

"Then it couldn't have been an invader," Adithya said.

"Unless it needed attention the dead Nepentheans could no longer provide."

"So," Tordor said, "we know no more than we knew from the beginning. Except that the silence was because the Nepentheans were dead."

"Not a meaningless discovery," Riley said. "But that's not all." He held up the bundle of material that once had been the suit the red sphere had provided for him, that had nourished him and protected him in the toxic Nepenthean environment. "There's a Nepenthean bone in the sample pocket, still safely secured. It can be tested for disease if we can find a safe place to test it and a way to do it."

"Perhaps your alien ship will provide for that as well," Tordor said.

Sarcasm was not a Dorian specialty, but Riley thought that Tordor had picked up some subtleties of expression from his human contacts. "That wouldn't surprise me," Riley said.

"Still, we have come a long way and risked a great deal for very little," Tordor said. "It does not bode well for our project."

"That's not all," Riley said.

"What more?" Tordor asked.

"There's this," Riley said, and he leaned toward the wall and traced a series of lines on the ruby wall with a fingernail.

"And what is that?" Tordor asked.

"It was on the front of the transparent wall," Riley said. "At first I thought it was marks made by the creature inside trying to get out. And then I saw that the marks were embedded inside the glass, as if they were a message to those in the hall."

"They look like scratches to me," Adithya said.

"And they may be, but they also may be connected to the death of the Nepentheans. We just have to decipher them, if they are a message," Riley said.

"They don't look like any written language I've ever seen," Tordor said. "And I have seen a great many."

The medallion on Asha's chest spoke for the first time since Riley's return. "This is something I was created to do," it said. "I cannot understand it now, but perhaps we will find more examples and I can compare them."

They looked at the scratches on the wall. They were fading now and soon they would be gone, but the Pedia would remember them and Riley and Asha, and they would linger in memory as they crossed the long reaches of empty space toward their next silent world.

CHAPTER SEVEN

The red sphere emerged from the nexus point and began the long journey to the focus of their next world of mysterious silence. The sun was a typical yellow star about the same age as Earth's sun, but it had accreted only half a dozen planets plus the usual collection of debris in various shapes, sizes, and orbits. There were the customary gas giants and then rocky planets with varying degrees of size and atmospheres, but only one was in the Goldilocks zone where water was liquid, and it was a super-Earth, three times the size and weight of the human birth world but, Tordor said, just about the right size for Dorians. He found this a reason to claim the right to explore the world, so like his own, that had stopped communicating with the rest of the Federation.

"All of you would be seriously handicapped down there," Tordor said. "You would drag along, one slow step in front of another, if you could even walk. I grew up in conditions like these. It would be like returning home."

"You haven't been on a high-gravity world since you were a young adult," Asha said. "Your muscles are no better than ours."

"It is true that my strength has been diminished by the effete conditions in which I have had to work," Tordor said, "but mine has the potential to regenerate, which cannot be said for any of you."

So the debate went between the ordinary dull daily activities aboard the alien ship, eating, resting if seldom sleep for the transcendents, long naps for the untranscended son of Earth, terrifying, experience-defying moments of transition between space and the nonspace of Jumps through the nexus points that lay in a scattered pattern across the galaxy, navigating between almost forgotten points of entry, and emergence hundreds of light-years away. Adithya had to be restrained the first few times as the reality of their spaceship world was transformed into something unrecognizable, but even he had become accustomed to not being able to recognize his surroundings or his fellow travelers or even the report of his senses.

In the midst of all the essential aspects of space travel in the age of the Galactic Federation, they had a chance—indeed, the necessity—to talk: about their mission, about their lives, individual and shared, and about their disagreements. The Pedia had not been able to decipher the Nepenthean scratches, if they were a method of writing rather than accidents or the decay of time. It needed more examples, if the message was a message and if it was connected to the destruction of the Nepentheans. Tordor did not think there was any purpose in pursuing such fragments of an unrealizable possibility, and Riley insisted that evidence accumulated until it settled into a recognizable pattern and that it was too early to dismiss anything.

The Pedia had managed to establish a limited connection to the mind or minds that controlled the red sphere, that responded to its physiological analysis of its occupants and adjusted its shape and function to their needs. It had been an intuitive process for Riley from the moment he had entered it on the planet of the dinosaurs where he had been stranded by the Transcendental Machine, but sometimes those intuitions went awry and now the Pedia could sometimes request specific actions and sometimes get appropriate responses.

"I still cannot understand the millions of tiny voices that seem to make up the mind of this ship," the Pedia said. "Perhaps it is because they all speak at once."

"Or maybe," Tordor said, "they exist only in your imagination."

"I have no imagination," the Pedia said.

One of the actions the Pedia requested for them was an analysis of the bone Riley had recovered from Nepenthe. "The bone displays no evidence of poison or bacteria other than the natural products of an environment that most carbon-based life would find toxic," the Pedia reported.

"It could have been a fast-acting poison or microbe that did not have time to reach the bone," Tordor grunted.

"That's true," Riley said, "and any such traces might have washed away if the Nepentheans were floating or immersed in fluid, as I suspect."

"We work with what we have," Asha said. "Meanwhile, we must consider what answers this next world may have for us."

"We call it Centaur," Tordor said. "Or, to be more precise, the land of the Centaurs." He did not use the human word, which he did not know, but a word that in Galactic Standard described a creature that had four legs and a torso that grew out of the creature's forebody with arms at the shoulders and something on top of the shoulders that resembled a head.

"A centaur," the Pedia said, and explained to Asha, Riley, and Adithya, who had never been exposed to mythology, what the ancient Greeks had imagined, and it created on a wall of the dining area a reproduction from its seemingly unlimited store of images.

"An improbable creature," Tordor said, "but, given the vast galaxy and the billions of planets it has birthed, life has had an opportunity to take improbable directions. Personally, I have never seen one, but then it is a young species, still an apprentice member of the Federation."

"How long has it been an apprentice?" Adithya asked.

"Only ten thousand long-cycles," Tordor said.

"Ten thousand!" Adithya said. "Ten thousand years ago—or, as you say, 'long-cycles'—my ancestors were still learning how to be farmers."

"And if your species had only accepted apprentice status," Tordor said, "the galaxy would have been saved a generation ten long-cycles of death and destruction."

No one had anything more to say, but they said a great deal anyway during the long trip from the nexus point through the solar system to the planet Centaur.

The red sphere landed gently on top of a small hill in the midst of a forest of thick-trunked, stunted trees like overgrown bonsai, a term that the Pedia had to explain. Everything was stunted here on the world that

Tordor had called Centaur, and the human occupants of the ship could feel the pull of the big world through the red walls that protected them from everything else.

"We can't stay long," Asha got out between breaks to breathe, "but the Pedia clone will remain in contact and tell us when you are ready to return, or if you need help."

"Though it's hard to imagine how we would be able to help," Riley said. "You were right. We'd be no good on a world like Centaur."

"I won't need any help," Tordor said, and, waving his trunk at Adithya through the protective suit the red sphere had extruded for him, pushed his way through the ruby wall and onto a surface he had not felt for some long-cycles since they had left Federation Central, and onto a world whose powerful tug, like a lover's embrace, he had not felt since he left Dor. For a moment, standing in crushed, mosslike vegetation, a little darker, bordering on purple, than his native world, Tordor felt his thick knees sag, but he straightened up and looked around. There were forests on every side of the hill and no indication which way to go. So, as the red sphere elevated behind him and dwindled into the thick atmosphere, he started down the hill toward the rising yellow sun.

By the time he reached the bottom of the hill—it was little more than a bump in what were otherwise fertile plains much like his native Dor—he was panting. But with each step he felt himself grow stronger, like a long-departed child returning home. His legs would feel leaden as soon as he had to rest, but they would recover.

He stopped under the shade of one tree. It had an enormous trunk and thick branches held tightly, as if resisting the attraction of the heavy planet. Even so, some of these massive trees had been toppled and lay strewn among their more fortunate fellows. Their roots, almost as thick and long as the branches themselves, reached into the air like pleading arms. Some of the trees still standing had globular fruits, yellow and red and purple, hanging from low limbs.

Tordor took a deep breath and then, impulsively, pushed his short trunk through the envelope of the red suit that enveloped his sturdy body from head to hoof.

The medallion hanging from a chain around his thick neck said, "Danger! Danger!"

"We'll soon find out," Tordor said and took another deep breath, this time of real air. Centaur smelled a bit like the oases of his youth on Dor but with a strong odor of strangeness that would take some getting used to, if he had the chance. But it was good, thick air, full of the clean smell of soil and purplish, growing things rather than the recycled breathings and other emissions of creatures confined together for long cycles. The red sphere worked remarkable magic on the air within the ship, but it could not eliminate the odors of close alien contact. He began stripping the envelope from his body and ended with his trunk holding a bundle of red material that he stowed away in the pouch around his waist.

"Even if there are no deadly gases in the air," the Pedia said, "there are bacteria and viruses for which you have no immunities."

"The Federation inoculates everybody against all known pathogens," Tordor said. "Otherwise we could never tolerate contact with a new species. If you were not an immature Pedia from a primitive planet, you would know all that."

"You may ridicule my experience and my world," the Pedia said, "but you should not endanger the mission."

"We need to develop a working relationship," Tordor said. "You keep quiet until asked, and I won't dispose of you on this alien world."

"You will need me to get in touch with the ship," the Pedia said. "And no matter what you think now, you may need me before our stay on this world is finished."

"If I need your help, I will ask for it," Tordor said. "And if I get rid of you, I can always return and dig you up if I need to contact the ship."

The Pedia was silent, and Tordor threaded his way between the trees and the fallen trunks until he got a glimpse of the rolling grasslands beyond.

"Danger! Danger!" the Pedia shouted.

Almost coincident with its warning the world began to shake. Tordor was thrown to the ground. It was a savage blow in these gravitational conditions, and he lay there groaning for moments until he pushed himself up to his knees and upper limbs, bracing himself against the shuddering land under him. He staggered to his hooves and looked around at the thrashing trees, trying to remain upright. A tree toppled in the distance with a sound like a clash of giants. Tordor imagined that

massive growth being torn from the ground and the force that it took to bring it down.

"We should leave this location immediately," the Pedia said. "We are experiencing a shifting of geologic plates, what we called on Earth an 'earthquake,' but here, I suppose—"

"A centaurquake," Tordor said. He ran, or tried to run though it turned out to be more of a staggering trot, through the thrashing trees until he was in the grassy plains beyond. By then the ground had settled down. He had never experienced a movement of the world beneath his hooves before, and it disturbed him more than he was willing to admit, even to himself.

"Clearly," the Pedia said, "this world, as massive as it is, has fault lines and maybe thinner plates than you experienced on Dor."

"Clearly," Tordor grunted, and would have said more, but just then he saw a centaur approaching, unshaken, from the far distance of the plain, and behind it came a group of centaurs like a herd.

They were not like the thin-legged quadrupeds the Pedia had illustrated on the walls of the ship. They were quadrupeds, clearly enough, but thick-bodied and thick-legged, and the torsos that grew from the shoulders of the creatures were short and thick as well, with two-jointed arms protruding from wide shoulders and a mouth and what seemed to be eyes in what seemed otherwise like a lump on top of the torso. And their skin or fur was purplish, like the vegetation.

"More like a hippopotamus than a horse," the Pedia said. It told Tordor about the Earth animal that had once lived in rivers and ponds on Earth before it and other wild animals had been eliminated during the early twentieth centuries by overhunting, the loss of habitats to encroaching human invasions, and the climate changes that preceded Pedia supervision.

"Your world was indeed barbarous," Tordor said.

"It went through growing pains," the Pedia said, "like every world that survives industrialization. The transition is as difficult as that following the fall of massive meteorites. But these are the dominant species on this world?"

Indeed, they seemed more like herd animals and without the normal herd-animal wariness about potential predators. They had no tools, no weapons, no clothing or adornments. They came straight toward the edge of the forest, ignoring the bulky figure of Tordor standing in the grassy meadow just outside the forest edge, and began reaching into the lower-hanging branches for the fruit Tordor had noticed earlier. Some of it had fallen to the ground during the centaurquake and been smashed, but a good deal was still remaining and the centaurs clearly were gorging themselves, apparently undisturbed by the recent disturbance in the surface beneath their hooves.

They were not grazers, then, as Tordor's people had been. They were fruit eaters, and it was hard to believe that creatures such as these had built a civilization and spaceships and had ever been considered for membership in the Federation. "Maybe they're wild ones that have never been civilized," Tordor said. "Or left untouched by civilization as test subjects or evolutionary reserves. There are such on Dor."

"It is difficult to imagine any creatures like these coexisting with scientists and engineers," the Pedia said.

"We are searching for the consequences of a catastrophe that has engulfed this part of the galaxy," Tordor said. "Maybe this is one of them."

He approached a nearby centaur and spoke to it in Galactic Standard. The creature seemed to glance at him, though it was difficult to tell where its eyes were looking, and then continued eating the fruit in its hand.

"We do not seem to be making any progress," the Pedia said.

"For a Pedia you are remarkably impatient," Tordor said.

"On an expedition like this," the Pedia said, "speed and quick decisions are essential. You have failed to notice, for instance, the approach of another species."

Indeed, Tordor had not seen the creature approach from the rear of the herd. It was thick, like all the other creatures on Centaur, but lithe and colorful, with a brown coat or skin and gold stripes, a massive head with a large mouth from which two long teeth projected from the top of its jaw over a lower lip. And it moved with the slow, tense movements of a predator, its head rigidly focused toward a smaller centaur at the back of the herd, perhaps an immature member of the group.

"That creature resembles an Earth-born predator called a saber-toothed tiger, of which there were at least two different evolutionary types," the

Pedia said. "They both became extinct long before humans swung down from the trees to walk the savannas. Other predators evolved, other tigers, panthers, lions, wolves, but they all disappeared in the great—"

"Now is no time for lessons in pointless human evolutionary history," Tordor said.

The tiger-creature had broken its stealthy, paw-after-paw approach with a sudden dash that dropped the trailing centaur with a single savage thrust of long front teeth into the rear of the centaur's spine and then a quick shift to the head of the torso that left the victim bleeding, lifeless on the meadow next to the forest. The tiger-creature looked around. The other centaurs continued to pluck fruit from the trees, undisturbed. The tiger-creature sank its teeth into the haunch of the centaur and began pulling it away.

For a moment Tordor was silent, as if stunned by the savagery of the world and the apparent lack of response from its once-dominant species. Then he said, "If these centaurs were once civilized spacegoers, they aren't any longer. If we have any chance of finding some who are, we will have to look elsewhere."

But before he could turn away, he saw another tiger-creature stalking from the far end of the meadow toward the heedless herd. He looked around, picked up a fallen branch in his trunk, and moved as quickly toward the predator as the gravity allowed.

"This is folly!" the Pedia said. "You are not the kind person who risks his life for another creature."

"I feel strange stirrings of compassion," Tordor said. He did not stop.

"Transcendence," the Pedia said, "means becoming more rational. Not more emotional."

But Tordor could not be stopped, and he brought the improvised club down on the head of the tiger-creature at the moment it crouched to begin its charge toward a centaur. Like the centaurs, it had grown unconcerned about dangers but perhaps for different reasons. After a moment the creature staggered to its feet and slunk away, looking back once over its shoulder to see if it was being followed.

"Now," Tordor said, "we can go on. The city is that way. If there is any remnant of centaur civilization, it will be there."

"You are going in the wrong direction," the Pedia said.

CHAPTER EIGHT

The red sphere was not the same without Tordor's substantial presence. Not much taller than Riley but several times heavier, he occupied space with his body as well as his experience of command. Asha was always conscious of where he was and what he was thinking, and when he was not there she felt liberated. She did not tell Riley that, but she knew, with the unspoken communion that had only grown stronger between them since they first met in the waiting room on Terminal, that he felt the same way, only in a more masculine, competitive fashion.

Adithya, on the other hand, seemed to miss the big, pachyderm-like alien.

They had ascended to a stationary orbit some thousands of meters above the spot where Tordor had pushed through the red sphere's yielding surface onto the Centaur hill. They were still in the control room and the Pedia embedded in the medallion around Asha's neck had kept them updated on Tordor's exploration, including alarm when Tordor had sampled the Centaur air and even greater alarm when he had removed the protective suit the red sphere had fashioned for him.

"I would have thought his transcendence would have given him better judgment," Riley said.

"He has been confined with us in this colorful prison for a long-cycle," Adithya said. "He could not resist the opportunity to breathe air that has not been recycled millions of times and contaminated with the body odors of humans and the odd scents of unfamiliar food. Besides, if his stay is extended, his air supply might not last."

"I went through the same experience on Nepenthe," Riley said.

"But you didn't have the option of removing your suit," Adithya said. "The air was poisonous. And Tordor had the further temptation of a world much like the one on which he was born. It must have been like coming home."

"Let's not get sentimental about Tordor," Asha said. "He wouldn't appreciate that."

"The centaur world seems to be unstable," the Pedia said. "The ground is shaking and Tordor has been thrown down."

"Has he been hurt?" Adithya said. "At that gravity—"

"He is not hurt, but he is moving more carefully."

A few moments later, the Pedia said, "Tordor has seen his first centaurs, and they do not appear to be concerned about his appearance. In fact, they have ignored him and are going about their regular eating practices. They are fruit eaters."

"Has he tried to communicate with them?" Adithya asked.

"He does not know their language," the Pedia said, "so he has tried Galactic Standard without success. In any case they are not paying attention to him or to anything else, including a predator that is approaching them."

"I hope Tordor has seen the predator and is staying out of its way," Adithya said.

"He is a Dorian warrior," Asha said, "with experience as a commander and the advantage of transcendence as well."

"The predator has attacked and killed one of the centaurs," the Pedia said, "and a second predator is approaching. Tordor is reacting peculiarly. He has attacked the second predator. Successfully, it seems. The centaurs seem unconcerned by all this. There is some doubt about their intelligence or the absence of instinctive awareness of danger."

"They are not dead like the Nepentheans," Riley said, "but maybe something inside their brains has died."

"Tordor is heading toward the nearest city," the Pedia said. "He should have more information soon."

With no updates likely to be forthcoming for some time, Adithya left the control room to get something to drink from the dining wall the red sphere had provided, leaving Asha and Riley alone. They were not alone much in the limited spaces provided by the red sphere, even though Asha had communicated with it, in the peculiar, imperfect connection they had developed, that their sleeping quarters should be sealed off when both of them were inside.

"Have you thought about the transcendental process?" Riley asked.

"What do you mean?" She knew what he meant, but she knew from experience that it was better if he said it.

"Tordor has been through the Transcendental Machine," Riley said, "but he seems little changed."

"He is a Dorian, and a very confident Dorian at that," Asha said, "but he seems more open about his past and less devious about his motivations."

"'Seems' is the operative word."

"And yet he attempted to protect Adithya," Asha said.

"If it was not his deviousness reasserting itself."

"And, apparently, he has been moved, quixotically, to protect the centaurs."

"Which speaks to the appearance of a new emotion, compassion, if not to an old one, rationality."

"And yet?" Asha prompted.

"It makes one wonder about the transcendental process itself," Riley said. "Is the person who gets reconstituted in the receiver the same person who gets analyzed and transmitted in the Transcendental Machine?"

"Clearly not," Asha said. "The imperfections are left behind."

"And what else?"

Asha nodded. "Are we the same people, minus the flaws that keep us from the ideal version of ourselves? Or are we new creatures with the memories of our old selves attached?"

"Yes," Riley said. "My transcendental version shouldn't have such debilitating concerns."

"Do they keep you from acting when action is necessary?"

"No. At least I don't think so."

"Are your feelings any less real? Are they like someone else's memories or do they still cause physiological reactions? Do you remember your life growing up on Mars, your mother, your father, your first love."

"And what happened to them. And the anguish that caused me. But in a way that allows me to cope with it, to make me stronger rather than weaker."

"Then perhaps it doesn't matter," Asha said. "Except in theory."

"And the way we feel and act in practice," Riley said.

Asha knew that this was true and that Riley believed it and that, in spite of all, the doubt lingered. But it was the existential doubt that hung over all conscious life: reality or dream, flesh and blood or shadows cast on a cave wall, actuality or scenarios being enacted in some immense computer? They would have to live with uncertainty and act as if it did not exist.

When Adithya returned to the control room, he asked if the Pedia had reported anything new about Tordor and seemed relieved that nothing had happened. He looked around as if looking for answers somewhere else. Asha thought it was a symptom of his attachment to the Dorian, as if he had transferred his allegiance from Latha to the most authoritative figure nearby.

Adithya looked at the viewplate that served them in every way that connected them to the galaxy outside the ship. "Look!" he said. "There's that unidentified object again, in the upper left-hand corner, a red dot that Tordor said might be a ship."

"Or just an uncharted body," Riley said. "This ship's database—whatever it is and wherever it is located—is a million years old."

"This is where we need Jak's machine," Asha said. "Our mission would be so much simpler if we could communicate instantly with Federation Central or a hundred other possible sources."

"And additional transcendents," Riley said.

"Do you think Jer can be successful in persuading the Federation to adopt the machine and scatter replicas across this spiral arm?" Adithya asked.

"It won't be easy," Asha said. "In spite of the obvious advantages of instant communication across interstellar distances, it means a major change in the way the Federation functions. And change means that people who have an investment in the status quo are in danger of losing their positions of authority and those who might gain by it are uncertain how it will work out."

"And there is the natural resistance of the bureaucracy," Riley said. "And maybe the Federation Central Pedia, which dislikes change even more than the bureaucrats. And this doesn't begin to account for the resistance of people to transmitting themselves, much less the thought of personal destruction and re-creation."

Sometime later the Pedia reported, "Tordor has entered the centaur city."

CHAPTER NINE

Jer inserted the capsule into the round slot in the control panel in front of her and closed and locked the door that kept it in place. Before she pressed the button that would conclude, and she hoped culminate, the work that had brought her to Federation Central, she looked around the cluttered, improvised space the Federation had assigned to her.

Her Federation Central laboratory was nothing like her father's laboratory on the dark side of Earth's moon. That was a fully functional and extensively equipped facility with computer coordination and computation—not a pedia, with its intrusive questions and subversive monitoring, and certainly not a Pedia—and some special instruments invented by her father.

Actually—and her father had taught her to think in the kind of precise, accurate terms that enabled humans to live independently in a Pedia-dominated world—Jak was not her father but the person from whom she and her brothers and sisters, now all dead but her, had been cloned. But it was a waste of time—and Jak had taught her that every moment in the search for truth was precious—to refer to herself as a clone and Jak as the person of whom she was a biological copy. And there was the familial relationship, strained almost beyond endurance when she and her fellow clones had been exiled at an early age to a satellite orbiting a moon of Jupiter, contaminated by an organism that they had developed to retain Ganymede's warmth, and the only one brought back to work with Jak while Jon and Jan were sent off to join the voyage of the *Geoffrey* to search for the Transcendental Machine. And there were those moments under the lash of Jak's paranoid intensity when she could appreciate how he drove himself with the same desperate urgency of his race against extinction before he had solved the universe's riddles, and a cherished few when his long-buried humanity broke through and he could almost evidence tenderness. And there was the year after Jak's first trial of the teleportation device he had reconstructed from Riley's description when Jak's first experimental subject had been Jer and his second himself, and just as she had shed the symbiotic mantle she had worn since its unwelcome partnership with Jak, his health and even his years restored, had lost his fear of death before victory and seemed almost fatherly.

Moreover, this was not quite Federation Central but a barren companion world with abandoned structures where, she had learned from Asha during the long voyage from Earth, prisoners captured from the first human extrasolar voyages had been imprisoned and questioned for decades before the human/Federation war. Federation Central was not only secret but sacred, not to be contaminated by uninvited guests, and its scientists, and most of all its Pedia, suspected researchers not under their control of preparing noxious or explosive materials. But with the help of a few antique machines and a surly Pedia she had restored one structure into an adequate facility in which to create a replica of her father's machine. Now had come the time to display it—to prove to the Federation representatives that the machine worked, that it could solve the Federation's problem of communicating with its distant member worlds and, although it would not be apparent for some time, would create a new generation of transcendents to transform their species and the Federation.

The machine her father had built was not quite the legendary apparatus that Riley had described to them. Jak had taken those bare-bones possibilities and added features that appealed to his sense of symmetry, function, and style. To the larger space that seemed to be appropriate for an operator, Jak had added a message console with a receptacle to send and receive capsules along with a computer to receive and send verbal and digital messages, as well as a keyboard for identifying destinations. What the Transcendental Machine had lost over the million long-cycles since it was created was an instruction manual. Its means of controlling the destination of what it transported had been lost to the ages. Jak wanted the operation to be foolproof. Not only was he skeptical about the ability of others to follow simple directions, he also was cynical about their susceptibility to attractive technology.

What Jak did not want to be obvious was that the space provided for an operator also was capable of being used as a transmission device. The Jak Machine—he had renamed it in order to distance it from the mythology that had grown up around the Transcendental Machine but also out of the remnants of Jak hubris—was capable of transporting living creatures, like its predecessor. Or rather their electronic equivalents, stripped to their ideal state while their previous incarnations were turned into dust by the computer that analyzed them as they were being destroyed. In that it was identical in means and purpose to what the Transcendental Machine had accomplished. But a million long-cycles later the desperation that had moved pilgrims to seek refuge in its enigmatic embrace was unavailable. The member species of the Federation would have to be convinced that the Jak Machine worked and that the benefits of instantaneous transmission across light-years were worth the perils of being destroyed. It was a sales pitch that would be difficult to make and even more difficult to make persuasive.

At the heart of the Jak Machine, buried in its base, was a small black box that contained the indispensable ingredient for the entire process, not the computer, not the analytic ray that disintegrated the subject, but the entangled particles separated from their mates in secure compartments and tagged in ways that they could be identified by the Jak Machine's computer. That was the indispensable contribution Jak had made to the machine Riley had described. The Transcendental Machine may have operated on the same principle, but how its creators had accomplished it was as mysterious as interaction-at-a distance itself, and Jak had to reinvent it and the means of separating the particles and yet making them addressable. Federation scientists could back-engineer the Jak Machine, but they couldn't open the black boxes without allowing the separated particles to escape. They would have to reinvent the process for themselves, and Jak didn't think they could do it. And if they wanted to try, they would find that it was easier and cheaper to get the black boxes from Jak.

Jak's psychological problems, along with his physical condition, had been improved by his passage through his machine, but it had not changed his character. He still was supremely confident of his ability to understand the universe, and he never doubted his superiority over any possible competition.

Jer pressed the button on the keyboard in front of her. When she opened the door that had sealed the capsule in place, the capsule was gone. Only dust remained to be vacuumed automatically when the door was closed again. She got out of the Machine and moved to its replica on the other side of the laboratory. She sat down in it and pressed another button. The capsule door swung open, but the space behind was empty.

Jer sighed. She still had work to do.

Thirty cycles later she told the Pedia that was supervising, or spying on, her operation that she was ready for a demonstration.

"I have observed the progress of your work," the Pedia said. "The appropriate scientists have been kept informed about its progress, although their interest, judged by their access to my reports, has diminished as time has passed without results."

"And yet you have seen it work," Jer said. She resented oversight by a Pedia and now she had to convince one that she had accomplished what she had promised.

"And I will so report," the Pedia said. "Although there are a number of alternative explanations for what your experiment demonstrates, and I should caution you that convincing Federation scientists of results that their science tells them is impossible will be difficult."

"Nothing's easy," Jer said. She had learned that bit of wisdom from Riley. He had applied it to learning Galactic Standard, which she had accomplished during the long trip to Federation Central.

The deputation that arrived, fifty cycles later, was a single, sullen

Xiforan, a junior scientist who would be least missed on Federation Central and whose report, Jer knew, would be least regarded. Nevertheless, she prepared the demonstration as if she were going to present it to a senior delegation.

"You may inspect the message to be sent across the workshop"—she did not want to demean the term by calling it a "laboratory"—"to the unit on the other side." She held out the message she had handwritten on a piece of paper. Paper was virtually nonexistent on Federation Central, and she had torn a sheet from her notebook.

The weasel-like Xiforan glanced at it without giving it the respect of a careful examination.

"I'm going to place it in this capsule," Jer said. "The capsule is flimsy because it is used only to contain the message and will be destroyed."

The Xiforan looked more interested when she said the Galactic Standard word for "destroyed."

Feeling already that she was wasting her time as well as boring the Xifor, Jer sat down in the Jak Machine, inserted the capsule into the receptacle for it on the control panel, and pushed the button that closed the door. "Now, I'm going to push this button that will initiate the process," she said. She pushed the button. A muffled hissing sound came from the control panel. She opened the door to the round slot.

"You see?" she said. "Only dust."

"You have invented an incinerator!" the Xiforan said, with what might have been irony in a human.

"Come with me," she said, and after getting out of the Jak Machine she led the way to the machine on the other side of the workshop. She sat down and opened an identical capsule door. Behind it was a capsule. She held it up to the Xifor, who looked not so much startled by the revelation as surprised that this would seem remarkable. Jer opened the capsule and showed the piece of paper to the Xifor with the message she had written. "See?" she said. "The message I showed you over there."

"How do I know you did not write the message twice and leave one here to be discovered?" the Xiforan said.

"Perhaps I should have started in a different place," Jer said. "But you didn't seem"—she was going to say "interested" but decided to change it—"involved. Here. Write something down on this sheet of paper."

"Xifora do not write," the Xiforan said.

"Make a mark—something only you are aware of," Jer said. "Insert it in the capsule and put the capsule into that round space. I'll turn my back."

When she turned around again, the Xiforan was inserting the capsule. "Close that little door with the button beside it," she said, "and then push that button." She pointed to the button on the other side of the panel. The Xiforan wedged itself into the machine, and Jer gave herself a mental note to make the bench adjustable. The Xiforan pushed the button. "Now open the capsule door," Jer said. "The button beside the little door opens it, too." The capsule door opened. There was only dust behind it.

"Now come with me," she said, and led the Xiforan to the machine from which they had started the experiment. "Now open the capsule door." The Xifor slid into the seat—more skillfully this time—and pushed the button beside the door. Behind the door was the capsule. "Open it," she said. The Xiforan opened the capsule and removed the sheet of paper. It looked at the paper with something approaching awe.

"That's a great trick," it said. "How did you do it?"

At the end of a dozen more trials, the Xiforan seemed convinced that something other than trickery—of which it claimed to be an authority—was involved. "You may be able to send a message across the room," it said, "but I can speak loud enough to be heard, or, even better, use a communication device to serve the purpose more quickly and with far less equipment."

"The virtue of the machine," Jer said, "is that it works across any distance, to the farthest worlds of the Federation as quickly as it works across the room."

"Ah," the Xiforan said, "and how do you plan to prove that?"

"Send one of the machines to Federation Central," she said, "and I will demonstrate that the millions of kilometers that separate these worlds are no more significant than the few meters across the room."

The Xiforan submitted its report to the scientific committee of the

Federation Council that had sent it. Jer did not think the committee would respond, but perhaps it would give more weight to the Pedia's evaluation. And so it proved. Five cycles later the Pedia announced that the committee had given permission for one of the machines to be shipped to Federation Central, on the assurance of the Pedia—it did not mention the Xiforan—that the machine contained nothing toxic or explosive.

Fifty cycles later the machine had arrived on Federation Central and the committee had been assembled in a carefully prepared laboratory equipped with two-way vision screen communication monitored by the Pedia. Communication, however, was handicapped by the eight-minute delay caused by the distance between the two planets. "Proceed with your demonstration!" one of the committee members said. Jer was sure it was the director of the committee: it was a Dorian.

Jer went through the same series of demonstrations that she had performed for the Xiforan but with the improvements suggested by the Xiforan's reactions to the first tryout. She persuaded the Dorian to write a message, insert it in a capsule, and send it off. Eight minutes later she reported that the capsule had arrived and asked the Xiforan to read the message back.

"Xiforans do not read," it said. Jer read the message aloud.

Eight minutes later the Dorian responded that the message was correct. "However," it said, "it would have been just as quick to send a message by more customary methods."

"What you did not take into account," Jer said, "is that your message was received as soon as you sent it, and it was only the built-in delay of more customary methods that made the report take longer."

"So," the Dorian said, "your machine, if it works as you say, buys us eight minutes."

"Not only eight minutes," Jer said, "but eight light-years or eighty or eight hundred, or as far as the Federation can reach."

"A statement that would take many long-cycles to demonstrate," the Dorian said.

"But one that, if true—and it is easy to prove that instantaneous over the millions of kilometers that separate our two planets would be the same over light-years—would revolutionize Federation communication and bring the farther worlds into a new and intimate connection with Federation Central."

Communication with the committee over eight-minute breaks was like a conversation in which each of the parties took short naps between statements, and Jer found it beyond annoying, and perhaps disastrous.

At last the response came. "We cannot rule out the possibility of illusion. We are aware of the human fondness for trickery of the senses, something the rest of the Federation finds disturbing and perhaps infantile."

"What can I do to convince you that the process works and that it could work to make the Federation a better organization," Jer said, feeling frustrated and that failure of her project—and more important, Jak's—was imminent.

"Even if everything you say were true," the Dorian said, "can you imagine the consequences of objects like this arriving at Federation Central ten times, a hundred times, a thousand times a cycle? And what mischief, what toxic substances, what explosives might be included? It would be a nightmare."

"Surely Federation ingenuity could come up with suitable arrangements," Jer said. "Messages could be received on a remote planet like this one and processed by your Pedia, or on a satellite, or an office in orbit. Or almost anything! Or you could confine communications to oral only—any, yes, the Machine is capable of that as well."

Eight minutes later, the Dorian's reply arrived. "We will take that under advisement."

Jer felt her hopes sink beneath the weight of bureaucracy. She knew what that meant. "Maybe we need to speak without this delay," she said and pushed another button on the control panel of the Jak Machine.

She materialized in the Jak Machine on Federation Central. "Like this," she said.

CHAPTER TEN

Tordor was tiring as he approached the area where the city might be located. Walking in the gravitational field of a heavy planet that reminded him of Dor in many ways was not the pleasant jaunt that he remembered from his youth, and his muscles ached. He also found himself looking behind at regular intervals to see if he had been pursued by saber-toothed predators or some other creature that had not yet evidenced itself. But there was nothing.

He was almost upon the city before he recognized it. At first it seemed like a rise in the purplish-green vegetation that coated the prairies, but as he got closer Tordor could see low walls and roofs that extended for kilometers in every direction. It was like no city Tordor had ever seen, appropriate perhaps for a species that spent its life close to the ground, and for a heavy world that made raising objects to heights not only difficult but dangerous. Even so, his people, the Dorians, were grazers on a heavy planet, and they had built tall cities in the highlands as if defying their limitations. Tordor thought about the advantages of hands over trunks. Dorians had coped with their handicaps by maximizing the capabilities of their one major tool in challenging the limitations of their origins. The centaurs, on the other hand, had to contend with a treacherous and unstable world: he had experienced another centaurquake as he made his way across the prairie toward this place. Two of those a day would make any builder choose stout walls and single-level structures.

Even so, some of the buildings had fallen, perhaps from the quakes, perhaps from lack of attention. The neglect suggested that the city had been abandoned.

Walls surrounded the city as if to keep out strangers or perhaps predators like the saber-toothed tigers that he had seen at the edge of the forest. Openings broke the symmetry of the walls every few kilometers, but they were sealed with heavy wooden gates that did not yield to his pounding, even from his heavy hooves, and, even if he could climb, he did not want to risk an injury or even death, which would surely result from a fall from a height of more than a body length on this world. He circled the walls looking for an opening until he finally found a gate that had been splintered and partially destroyed. The splinters bulged out, some of them opening into holes, which meant that the gate had been attacked from within.

He squeezed his body through one of the holes, which was only large enough after he had enlarged it with kicks from his hooves. Inside, he stopped. Scattered in front of the damaged gate were heaps of bones, and Tordor remembered Riley's account of the meeting hall on Nepenthe. Only here some of the bones were broken and appeared to bear the marks of teeth. Tordor imagined panicked centaurs, trapped inside a city they could no longer understand and from which they could not escape, trying gate after gate until they finally found one they could kick their way through—only to let into their sanctuary the saber-toothed tigers that waited for them on the other side.

Tordor made his way through the boneyard into a broad avenue between low, one-story buildings constructed of wood or prairie mud colored by the purplish green of the native vegetation, and occasionally a kind of orange metal with which he was not familiar. Most of the buildings were small units, like individual stables; a few—the metal ones— were larger and extended into the ground farther than they rose above it. They seemed to be working places, factories perhaps, and one seemed to be for the construction or storage of vehicles that moved on thick, metal legs. Another housed what seemed like the beginning of an airship or perhaps a spaceship, though of an unusual design perhaps meant to accommodate heavy quadrupeds.

The boulevards extending toward what seemed like the center of the city were intersected at regular intervals by avenues that curved in what might be complete circles. The centaurs were—or had been—a species concerned with precision, it seemed, and they had laid out their city, maybe all their cities, with geometric regularity, although, at the end, their disciplined minds had done nothing to save them from whatever had attacked. Bones were piled at the other gates to the city, still closed though dented by the blows of hooves. Here, though, the bones were still in heaps, unscattered, most of them without tooth marks, and the smell of decayed flesh still lingered, perhaps after it had been absorbed by the porous stones on which they lay. The tigers, apparently, had gorged themselves at the gate they entered or had reached the other gates after the bodies had decayed too much even for their tolerance for carrion.

The Pedia had been silent during the entire process of exploration, and finally Tordor said, "Are you still there?"

"Of course," the Pedia said.

"You haven't made any disparaging remarks."

"You told me you would ask for my help if you needed it."

"And a good thing, too," Tordor said, though he found the silence disquieting. "Though that hasn't stopped you before. I'm heading toward the center of the city where I may find a reason for what has happened to these unfortunate centaurs."

"Why do you call them unfortunate?"

"No species would have brought this condition upon itself," Tordor said, and took the next broad avenue that led into the heart of the city.

"The history of civilizations suggests otherwise," the Pedia said.

The buildings Tordor came upon were older, larger, and in greater disrepair as he grew closer to the center of the city. The centaurs had started with a village and built outward from it as their numbers and their technological abilities increased. The newer structures closer to the walls had been built with better materials than the reinforced mud, or cement, that the earlier centaurs had put up, while the older buildings had been reconstructed and reinforced, though not enough to resist the ravages of time and a quaking world. Toward what seemed to be city-center was a large area that sloped gently down to a raised section at the far end. The entire space was defined by a low wall. In this gravity even a low wall was a deterrent.

"A corral," the Pedia said. "An enclosure for quadrupeds in a natural amphitheater, like the theaters of the ancient Greeks."

"I don't understand any of that," Tordor said. "It looks like a place four-legged creatures would gather, where they could stand and be instructed or entertained."

"That's what I said," the Pedia said.

There were no bones, though, as there had been in the meeting hall Riley had entered on Nepenthe. If the centaurs had been gathered here to receive some message and instead had been attacked by some virulent disease from outer space or some equally deadly alien invaders, they had not died in their place as they had on Nepenthe. He would have to look elsewhere for answers.

Tordor turned his body slowly to survey the structures that surrounded the amphitheater, wondering which one looked like an administrative building where decisions might be made about the everyday rules and regulations that govern a city or a world. That's where the alarm would have been sounded, if there had been time for an alarm.

"That building looks like city hall," the Pedia said. "The one there behind the corral—beyond the gathering place."

Tordor did not ask how the Pedia knew what he was thinking. He did not want to know, nor did he want the Pedia to know that it bothered him, that the thought of the Pedia peering into his mind, unlikely as it seemed but not impossible, made him uncomfortable. Even, perhaps, to the point of carrying out his threat to throw the medallion away.

"You were looking in that direction," the Pedia said. "I apologize for breaching our agreement. You did not ask for my assistance."

Tordor would have felt better about that reassurance if it had not addressed his unspoken concerns. But he refused to show the Pedia any sign of weakness. He moved around the perimeter of the amphitheater toward the large, low building on its other side.

The wide doorway had no closure, no door to keep centaurs out or in, and the outer wall meant that there would be no predators to be concerned about. The corridor beyond, wide and flat to accommodate the bodies of bulky centaurs, was dark, but Tordor could see by reflected sunlight that it was empty. Doorways opened on either side, like offices for minor bureaucrats or clerks, also without doors. Tordor glanced into them as he passed. Some contained what seemed like stalls with a table at one end and sometimes equipment upon it, perhaps to record or transmit information.

At the far end of the corridor was a door, the first one Tordor had seen in this building. It seemed to be made from the curious dark metal of the factory buildings, ornamented by carvings or engravings of geometric figures constructed with the straight lines that dominated centaur minds. It didn't make any sense that it sealed an opening to the outside if there were none in what Tordor took to be the front. There was no handle or anything Tordor could wrap his trunk around.

"If you touch me to the obstacle," the Pedia said, "I may be able to direct it to open."

Tordor considered the offer and would have liked to have turned it down but saw no better choice. He extended the medallion and ran it around the perimeter of the door and then toward the center. Finally something inside the door clicked, and it swung inward. Beyond was a larger space with a larger stall and a larger flat platform or table attached to its front. But one side of the stall had been knocked to the floor and bones lay in a regular pattern in front of the door, as if whatever centaur official had occupied this office, if that is what it was, had forgotten how to open the door that had separated it from the others, a door that had provided a kind of authority to the person who worked behind it, and, in the end, doomed it, though only a few moments sooner than the others.

Tordor was about to turn away and have the Pedia open the door that had swung shut when they entered, but the Pedia said, "A device on the working surface might provide some clues to what happened here, in this room and on this world."

There was, indeed, an apparatus on the table, not unlike what Tordor had seen on other such tables, but larger and more complicated. "We could perhaps take it back to the ship for analysis," Tordor said. "It seems unlikely that we can do much with it here."

"Let me try," the Pedia said.

Tordor hesitated and then extended the medallion until it touched

the device. A moment passed, and then suddenly, unexpectedly, a cacophony of sound burst forth from somewhere above his head. Tordor
recoiled. "What's that? What's happening?"

The sound diminished to a more tolerable level. "It seems to be coming from this device to sound enhancers on the roof of this structure
and throughout the building," the Pedia said. "Radio waves are being
transmitted to other devices for reproducing sounds and perhaps to re-
ceptors in other locations in the city and perhaps elsewhere, probably
to inform and direct, though that does not seem to be the reason for its
present emission."

"Why would anyone make such noise?" Tordor asked.

"Humans call it music," the Pedia said.

"Loud or not so loud," Tordor said, "it's still noise, and it is an
affront to whatever evolution has provided for its creatures to hear its
enemies and listen to its friends."

"Humans have a curious affinity for sounds of a particular nature
with different rhythms created by different instruments created for the
purpose," the Pedia said.

"Another reason for humans to have accepted a lower status in the
Federation until they had become sufficiently civilized."

"It is, to be sure, a very unusual music," the Pedia said. "Full of strange
rhythms and stranger tonalities, a sort of ambiguity, a shifting from moment to moment—"

"Turn it off," Tordor said. "I find it repellent." He did not say so, but
the sounds were beginning to make him feel uneasy, perhaps even uncertain, which was the worst feeling a Dorian could have.

The sounds ceased. He removed the medallion from the device on
the platform at the head of the centaur's stall. "Let's get out of this place,"
he said. "There are no answers here, only more questions."

He applied the medallion to the door. It swung open, more quickly
this time. And he found himself facing a saber-toothed tiger.

Tordor stepped back and slammed the door before the tiger could
spring. Perhaps it was the influence of the sounds the Pedia had inflicted
upon him, but he did not like his chances with a predator when he
had no weapon.

"From the bruise on his head," the Pedia said, "I think this is the tiger you struck earlier in a rash moment of sentimentality."

"That is the difference between us," Tordor said.

"Apparently it has trailed us from the forest edge," the Pedia said, "perhaps in another act of sentimentality."

"Predators, like Pedias, are never sentimental," Tordor said. He looked around the room for a weapon. Perhaps the broken stall. He picked up a piece of rounded wood, smooth under the sensitive touch of his trunk. It was too big to swing, almost too big to lift, and he propped one end against a wall and stamped on it with his right hoof. The wood broke into two pieces, splintered at the ends that once had been in the middle. He picked up the smaller piece and swung it. It was an acceptable weapon—not ideal but passable.

"I do not like our chances," the Pedia said.

"Small chances are better than no chances," Tordor said. "Open the door." He applied the medallion once more, with one hoof braced against the door to hold it shut until he could release the medallion and pick up the improvised club once more. Something thudded against the door, jarring it against him. When it stopped, Tordor put his shoulder against the door and let it edge open a crack, his club elevated to a striking position before he suddenly slammed the door shut again and heard the lock click.

Outside the door were two tigers and another was padding down the corridor behind them. He turned back into the room, searching for another way out. Behind him the door thudded again, and he had the impression that the lock, or whatever was holding it shut, might not be up to the task of holding out three tigers.

"I have informed the ship about our predicament," the Pedia said.

"My predicament," Tordor said.

"We are in this together."

"You are only a communication device," Tordor said, still searching the room.

"Nevertheless—"

"We are wasting time," Tordor said "Our colleagues in the ship can't help me in this gravity. I should have brought a weapon."

"Heavy-planet creatures have a misplaced confidence in their abilities, no doubt based on their musculature and the density—"

"Enough of such racial analysis and more thought about our situation," Tordor said.

"Apparently you have not noticed that this room is smaller than the width of the building it apparently occupies," the Pedia said.

"That's true," Tordor said, looking around more thoughtfully.

"If there are instruments on top of this structure," the Pedia said, "there must have been some access for quadrupeds to place them there and to provide whatever maintenance they might require."

"Yes, I see that."

"They would need a ramp."

"Of course," Tordor said. "But it could be outside."

"Possibly," the Pedia said, "but that would be no help to us. On the other hand—"

"It better be here," Tordor said. "That wall looks promising." He took the medallion in his trunk and applied it to the wall to his left, the one that seemed to be nearer to the center of the room than the one on the right. He moved the medallion across the breadth of the wall without results, and then, recalling the height of the centaur arms above the quadruped shoulders, he moved the medallion up. Still nothing happened.

Tordor turned back toward the door and the bones that lay in front of it. He searched among them and the tattered pieces of cloth that might have served as garments until he saw something that glittered in the gloom. He picked it up in his trunk. It was a piece of the strange dark metal from which the door and some of the newer buildings have been shaped. He held it up to the medallion.

The left wall clicked and a piece of the wall detached itself from the ceiling, letting the light of the setting sun illuminate a widening portion of the room. It swung down until it came to rest at floor level. Now it was clearly, as the Pedia had speculated, a ramp, and, as the door behind was battered again, Tordor moved toward it as swiftly as the heavy-gravity world permitted, toiled up the ramp, and stood outside in the clean-smelling Centaur air, looking at the red sphere ship that had come to rest only a few meters away.

CHAPTER ELEVEN

For a Dorian, Tordor seemed remarkably out of breath and wordless as
he burst into the ship through the red surface that was permeable only
to creatures the ship recognized through a process that none of them
had been able to decipher. Asha and Riley waited for Tordor to resume
his natural air of infallibility and imperturbability, but Adithya was not
so patient. "What happened?" he asked in his native language, a dialect
descended from the Asian subcontinent, before switching to the Anglo-
American-derived second language common to all humans, and then
to Galactic Standard that he had acquired during his time aboard the
ship. "The Pedia kept us informed, but it speaks in Pedia-ese, all information and no emotion."

Tordor had regained his dignity after his hasty departure from
Centaur. "I must admit that my distrust of your immature Pedia was
overdone. Its help was essential and proffered in a timely fashion." He
removed the medallion from his thick neck and handed it to Asha with
an air of relief that seemed at odds with the generosity of his words.

"As for the centaurs," Tordor continued, "they seem to have lost their
higher mental functions, even their survival instincts. If this is the result
of an alien invasion, there are no signs of aliens, unless they have turned
into the predators I encountered and from which I had to escape."

"That doesn't seem likely," Riley said.

"Nor was it presented as a likely scenario," Tordor said. "The predators—the Pedia compared them to Earth's tigers—were effective at what they did, which was to prey upon the centaurs, but they did not display the higher levels of intelligence necessary to build and operate spaceships or, indeed, technology of any kind."

"So," Asha said, "was this an instance of a worldwide epidemic that attacked the entire centaur population? And are you, perhaps, a carrier?"

"That, too, is unlikely," Tordor said. "Unless it was narrowly tailored for specific portions of the centaur brain and no other centaur parts or the minds of other creatures. The tigers did not seem affected. And it seems to have occurred suddenly and universally, not the normal vectors of pathogens."

"Unless it was released in the atmosphere at numerous places simultaneously," Riley said.

"To make it more like what happened on Nepenthe?" Tordor said. "To be sure, there are resemblances: bones piled up in both places. But on Nepenthe, the Nepentheans seem to have died in place. The centaurs we found in their city died because they had forgotten how to open the gates, and herds roamed the grasslands and forests untouched except for their minds."

"Then what is it we can draw from this experience?" Adithya said. "I hope you did not risk your life for nothing."

"One possible explanation," Tordor said, "is that Nepenthe and Centaur were both attacked by the same force, whatever it was, but that it affected them differently. They were, of course, aliens of quite different origins and development, and even intellectual perceptions of the universe, and it is possible that their response would not have been identical."

"What kind of force could do that?" Adithya said.

"That is difficult to say," Tordor said.

"Except," Asha's medallion said, "the music that was broadcast from the centaur office at the time of the catastrophe."

"Music?" Asha said.

"Noise," Tordor said. "It is difficult to imagine that this would be more than an annoyance. In any case, we did not retrieve the device that created it."

"That seems like an oversight," Riley said.

"We were in a bit of a hurry," Tordor said. "The tigers were breaking through the door, and if they had succeeded they could have pursued us up the ramp to the roof."

"That is no problem," the Pedia said. "I can reproduce the sounds of the centaur device."

"Go ahead," Asha said.

"That might be unwise," Tordor said. He did not want to tell the others about the unsettled way the sounds had made him feel. "If it damaged the centaurs—"

"Is it dangerous?" Asha asked the Pedia.

"Not to me," the Pedia said. "I cannot speak to the more fragile neuronic systems of living creatures."

"Do we have a choice?" Riley said. "Go ahead."

The sounds began. They were strange sounds indeed. After a moment Adithya cried out, "Stop! It is making me feel very strange."

"Yes," Asha said. "Stop it until we can analyze this more fully."

The sounds stopped.

"Well?" Tordor said.

"It does resemble music, though created by minds that share little with ours," Asha said. "I can understand why you were concerned."

"That is not—" Tordor began.

"Clearly it affected Adithya more quickly," Asha said. "Maybe because he has not had our experiences."

"I am not inferior," Adithya said.

"Of course not," Asha said. "You are our touchstone, our test subject. Without you we would be crippled."

"I'm the canary in the coal mine?" Adithya said. It was a reference whose literal meaning had been lost. There were no more coal mines and no canaries. The Pedia had to explain.

"This music—these sounds, whatever they are—is one more clue to add to the evidence from Nepenthe," Asha said. "When we have enough, we may be able to come to a conclusion."

———

The long, seemingly interminable voyage between nexus points brought no breakthroughs to the enigmas that were Nepenthe and Centaur. The Pedia reported periodically that it lacked sufficient information to make deductions, and tensions between travelers developed, as they always did between people of different origins and temperaments forced to associate for extended periods. Asha and Riley could not be divided, but even Adithya and Tordor began to bicker over small matters like food and cleanliness and odors and manners of communication or its other side, silence.

Finally, however, a new solar system appeared in the control-room window that served multiple purposes of viewscreen, navigation, and control. It was a remarkably familiar system with a G0 sun, an orbiting collection of icy comets, failed worlds, and assorted rocks, several gas giants, two of them with rings and all with dozens of satellites, and three Earth-sized planets, one of them a little cold, another much too hot, and a third just about right. It even had oceans, continents, and islands, and the oceans were liquid. The only thing that kept Asha, Riley, and Adithya from thinking that they might have returned to their home system was that the world had only two small, insignificant moons. "Like Mars," Riley said. "Or like Mars before the terraforming sent them hurtling into the planet."

"The natives of this world," Tordor said, "are a lot like you as well."

"Humanoids?" Asha said.

"Remarkably similar," Tordor said. "Deceptively so. Lemnia even has a breathable atmosphere and tolerable microbes and viruses. It almost makes a person believe in convergent evolution."

"That similar conditions produce similar results?" Adithya said.

"But then one realizes that among the billions of planets in the galaxy, some will inevitably produce species that resemble each other, and some, with almost identical conditions, will bring forth creatures that share almost no features," Tordor said. "And in the billions of galaxies that make up the universe, it is almost inevitable that some species will be identical, even down to their histories."

"You speak in riddles," Adithya said.

"I didn't know you were a philosopher," Asha said, "as well as a military leader."

"We grazers have a long time to think about how the universe was created and how it evolved into the complex system we observe today," Tordor said.

"To ruminate, so to speak," Riley said. "But you said these people—"

"They called themselves Lemnians," Tordor said. He did not, of course, say "Lemnians," but that is how the Dorian gutturals got translated.

"You said that they were 'deceptively' like humans."

"They are a congenial species," Tordor said. "The Federation doesn't have many Lemnians in its Galactic Center—their system is isolated out here on the fringes of our spiral arm, and they do not always send representatives—but they have always been solid and reliable for thousands of long-cycles."

"Unlike humans," Riley said.

"Exactly. But this is another world that has fallen suddenly silent," Tordor said.

"Then I think it is my turn to check this out," Asha said. "The conditions are within my range of tolerance, and the circumstances are not threatening but they may require some social skills."

"You imply my social skills are deficient?" Riley said. Asha understood that he was joking, but it was true—his experience growing up on Mars and serving in the human/Federation war had not included a necessity to get along with anything but official orders, and he had not even been good at that.

"You've never had to adjust your behavior to the expectations of others, or even to understand their expectations," Asha said.

"That doesn't apply to me," Adithya said.

"That's true," Asha said, "and you will have your opportunity when you get a little more experience, but this time I want you to monitor the Pedia's reports and to be ready to assist if that is called for." She placed the second medallion around Adithya's neck as if she were conferring an award, and turned to the control-room window to begin their descent to the Lemnian world below.

———

Lemnia was as Earth-like as Tordor had described. Asha stood in a field of something like clover, breathing air scented with the odors of growing vegetation, though tinged with hints of exotic, even alien herbs, enjoying the feeling of a spring day under a benign morning sun. It was enough to make a space traveler question her commitment to a life of off-planet exploration. And then the Lemnians descended upon her on the wings of creatures that resembled giant birds.

The birds were like pigeons grown to the size of winged horses and the Lemnians sat upon them in what looked like makeshift saddles fashioned out of cloth. Together, birds and Lemnians, they seemed unthreatening but organized, like well-trained cavalry and their mounts. There were seven of each, and the riders dismounted lithely and surrounded her while the birds eyed the clover as if trying to discover edible insects.

The Lemnians wore nothing but trousers with legs cut off at the calf, apparently needing no protection except from contact with their saddles. They were obviously mammalian, although their breasts were lower on their bodies. They were remarkably humanoid, as Tordor had said, but a little off in proportions and limb joints as if they had been together by an impressionist artist; their heads were hairless with eyes, nose, and mouth in the proper place, but the eyes were too large, the nose too small, and the mouth too wide. Their skin was a pleasing copper color, and they had a distinctive smell to them, acrid but not altogether unpleasant.

All this Asha noted in a single survey as she stood in their midst, unmoving, as they surrounded her and began touching her clothing—a simple spacer's orange coverall—and then prodding at her with their six-fingered hands. "I'm a person like you," she said, knowing they would not understand but beginning the process of socialization that might lead to communication. They twittered among themselves, like the birds they used for transportation, and then twittered at her, as if they, too, recognized the function of vocalization in creating connection.

The medallion said nothing, though she was aware that the Pedia was analyzing the language, as she was. The Pedia was not customarily reserved in its interactions, but apparently it was aware that the Lemnians might be tempted to remove something that made sounds. As it was, the Lemnians fingered the medallion before they allowed it to remain around her neck.

"I'm a representative of the Federation," Asha said, in an unthreatening tone, using Galactic Standard in the hope that some linguistic memory might linger, "here to discover why Lemnia has fallen out of contact." They might not understand her words, even in Galactic Standard, but they might recognize its purpose.

They twittered among themselves again and then one of them took Asha's hand and tugged her toward a nearby bird, which crouched to the ground at their approach. The Lemnian indicated that Asha should get astride the creature, and when Asha hesitated, pulled more strongly toward the bird until Asha threw her leg over the bird's back, and the Lemnian swung itself up behind Asha and twittered at their mount. With labored effort under the double load, the bird lifted itself and took a couple of steps before launching itself into the air with a great fluttering of wings, followed by the other Lemnians on their birds. They turned together, like a flock, and headed into the rising sun. It was a unique and disturbing experience for Asha, as she soared with aliens through an alien sky, with an alien wind blowing past her, and an alien landscape flowing past hundreds of empty meters below. She clutched the edge of the cloth that served as a saddle, was grateful for the Lemnian arm around her waist, and hoped that she would not fall off.

By the time they reached their destination, Asha had become accustomed to soaring through the air supported only by flapping wings and held in place by the arm of the Lemnian behind her. Their destination was a city of soaring spires surrounded by smaller buildings and then larger, flatter structures, like warehouses or manufacturing sites, on the outskirts. Except for the means of transportation, it resembled a modern city on any civilized world, perhaps with superior taste in architecture and city planning.

Their destination was one of the taller structures in the center of the city. The birds landed, with their passengers, on the building's flat top, and when their passengers, including Asha, had descended, the birds walked into cages placed around the periphery of the rooftop. Cage doors slid shut behind them, and the birds began to peck at troughs of food: insects or large worms or grain, Asha couldn't make out which before she was hustled by the entire seven Lemnians toward a door set into a structure in the center of the roof. The door slid aside as they approached, the Lemnians formed a protective guard around Asha, three in front, one on each side, and two behind, and they descended lighted stairs into the building.

They went down several flights of stairs before they arrived at another door, which one of the Lemnians had to touch before it slid aside, and they moved as a group into a hallway with some kind of cloth covering over the floor, not quite a rug with nap to it but more than a thin covering, perhaps like the saddles on the birds. And then they were at another door that slid open, Asha was pushed through into a dark space, with a twittering from the Lemnians, ceiling panels began to glow, and the door slid shut behind her. She took stock of her situation. She was alone on an alien world with aliens who could not understand her. She looked around at what seemed to be living accommodations. The walls had pictures on them, paintings perhaps, although they changed as she looked at them and the scenes they depicted were strange, like a familiar scene observed through a distorting window. There was something in the middle of the room that looked like a bed, something beside it that resembled a chair, a doorway to another room that might be a bathroom or a kitchen—she would find out later—and a door to the hallway through which she had entered that had no handle or apparent way to open it.

"I want to speak to someone," she said. Perhaps the room was wired for sound, and whoever was listening would understand her need to communicate even if they did not understand what she was saying.

"You can speak to me," the medallion said.

"I know that," Asha said. "But I'm not sure that's a good idea. Someone might be listening or watching who might not appreciate or understand Pedias. In any case, you need to focus on analyzing the language."

"That may take some time. But if you want to unlock the door, try putting me in contact with it. Usually these closures have some electronic switch buried inside that senses the approach of authorized personnel. I am smarter than any automated relay."

"Not yet," Asha said. "We need to wait until we can communicate."

"The people on the ship are concerned about your welfare and are asking if you need help," the Pedia said.

"Tell them I'm fine," Asha said. "There's nothing here I can't handle." She hoped that was true. And she could always call for help as long as the Lemnians did not recognize what the medallion was or take a liking to it as a decoration.

But what she did not say was the question that had bothered her from her first encounter with the Lemnians: where were all the males?

CHAPTER TWELVE

The open doorway led to what was both a restroom and a kitchen. Apparently the Lemnians did not make the kind of distinctions between physical functions that humans did. On a shelf were grains stored in canisters and liquids that came out of a tap. Asha sampled them gingerly and, when they produced nothing more than mild intestinal upsets that her body soon handled, satisfied her limited hunger and thirst with occasional bites and swallows. She spent one lengthy period of several hours resting on the raised pallet that served as a bed. The room had no window, so she did not know whether the Lemnian day had turned into night, but her internal clock told her that it had not yet been half an Earth day since the red sphere had landed her on Lemnia, though it felt that a lot had happened.

She spent her time working on her memory of the Lemnians' vocalizations, trying to match the twitters to the actions that had accompanied them, and when she allowed herself to slip into slumber it was to allow her unconsciousness to put together information that her awake mind did not quite accomplish. Still, when the door opened and two Lemnians entered the room, she had not yet mastered any of the meanings of the twitters they directed at her. Those twitters had, however, to be instructions to come with them to wherever they were going to take her, and, as she followed them out of the door and down the hallway in the opposite direction from the one she had entered, she began to sense a meaning, a difference between twitters and the tone in which they were spoken.

When a door at the end of the hallway slid open for them as they approached, Asha twittered at her escorts in what she hoped was a statement that she would enter the room without their help. They turned to stare at her with expressions that she could not yet identify and then shoved her through the door. It slid shut behind her.

The room was larger than the one she had occupied and clearly intended for an office rather than living quarters. It had a table inset with transparent panels. Other panels occupied spaces on the walls. They were all dark, as if the sources that had provided information to them had stopped working or the energy that fueled them had broken down. Benches lined each side of the room. A Lemnian sat behind the desk. Her body was heavier than those of the bird-riders who had first encountered Asha, and her coppery skin had a few lines in it. She smelled a bit more acrid than the bird-riders.

The official, if that was what she was, twittered at her. There was a question embedded in the statement, something like "What are you doing here?" Or, since she still wasn't sure she wasn't only guessing, she responded in Galactic Standard. "I'm here as a representative of the Federation."

The person behind the desk made a facial expression that may have been dislike or distrust and replied, in halting Galactic Standard, as if it were a language being recalled from childhood, "And what is the Federation?"

"The Galactic Federation," Asha began and then hesitated. Either the official was testing her or she had forgotten a great deal. "The Galactic Federation is an organization of different species in this arm of the galaxy."

"You speak in riddles, using words that have no meaning. Like 'galaxy' and 'arm.'"

"If you have forgotten—" Asha began.

"I have forgotten nothing but this wretched language," the official said, "which comes off the tongue in a barbarous manner."

"Let us begin again," Asha said. "I am Asha, a visitor to your world, come to find out more about your people and your way of life."

"What part of Lemnia are you from? And what are your reasons for coming here? You are not like any Lemnian I have ever seen. Were you born deformed? Or all your people like you?"

"I came from off this world," Asha said, "and where I came from people are much like me, with variations in size, color, and gender." She was a bit tired of standing before this—what, immigration officer? Jailer? Governor?—like a petitioner or a criminal. But she was not going to lose the advantage of height by sitting on one of the benches.

"What does that mean, 'off this world'?"

"I came down in a ship."

"A sailing ship?"

"A spaceship."

"That has no meaning. You came from the sky?"

"Yes," Asha said. "I came from the sky."

"Like the other sky people?" the official said.

"There were others?"

"The gods came back."

"Gods?" The Lemnians had retreated into ancient superstitions.

"Gods," the Lemnian repeated. She seemed to think for a moment. "You mentioned gender. That is another word that has no meaning."

"Where I came from, from the sky," Asha said, "there are males and females, each kind essential to the process of creating new people—babies who grow up into adults. And that brings me to a question I've been wanting to ask."

"Yes?"

"Where are your males?"

"We have no males," the Lemnian said. It seemed like the termination of a conversation, an interview, or an interrogation, whatever it had been. And Asha wasn't sure if she had passed or failed.

Behind her the door slid open and the two younger Lemnians entered, summoned by a means Asha had not noticed. Asha shook off their hands, turned, and went back down the corridor to the door from which she had left less than half an hour before. It opened in front of her and she went through into the room that seemed much smaller now. The door slid shut behind her.

"Is it time now to call for help?" the Pedia said.

"Not yet," Asha said. "First we need to do a little exploring. These people have forgotten a great deal, but I think they know something they are hiding."

She waited an hour before she applied the medallion to the door. It clicked and swung open. The corridor outside was empty. She moved slowly and quietly down the hallway. There were closed doors on each side. She put her ear to each one but heard no sound from the room behind the door until she reached the door to a room from which she heard a moan or groan. She applied the medallion to the door.

"Do you think this is wise?" the Pedia said.

"We need information," Asha said softly. "Don't make any noise."

The door clicked and slid open. The room behind was dark. Asha heard a twitter, then a burst of twitters, a little lower in pitch than any she had heard before. As she entered the room, ceiling panels glowed and then brightened. The room was almost identical to the one in which she had been imprisoned, but the raised pallet in the center had been replaced by a padded table. On the table, held down by straps, was a Lemnian, and not only a Lemnian but a male Lemnian. She could tell he was male because he was naked and his genitalia were exposed. They were not quite human genitalia but recognizable. He was looking at her with an expression that she thought might be a mixture of surprise and apprehension.

The male twittered at her. It sounded like a question.

"This Lemnian wants to know who and what you are and what you are doing here?" the Pedia said.

Clearly the Pedia had done more with the Lemnian language than she had. "Tell him—he is male by the way—that I am here to help him, but first I must have some information."

The Lemnian had looked at Asha with greater surprise when the medallion began to speak and seemed almost to faint when it addressed him in twitters. His body was thin, thinner than the bodies of the sturdy Lemnians who had escorted her to the city. He looked sick.

"Ask him—" she began, and then continued, "No, I will ask him myself." Suddenly, as such things happen, the language had fallen into place. "Do you want to have your bonds released?" she twittered. She moved toward the table.

"No," the Lemnian said. "Who are you? What do you want? You're not one of them."

"A Lemnian? No. I'm—from the sky," she said.

"A god?"

"There are no gods. I am a person like everybody." Well, except Pedias, she thought. "I came from a far-off world to find out what has been happening here on Lemnia."

"You don't look like everybody." The Lemnian was regaining his composure.

"I look like people from my world," Asha said. "Like you with a few differences caused by the way we evolved." She could find no Lemnian twitter for "evolved" and substituted "the gods made us."

"There are no gods, you said," the Lemnian twittered, and then, more somberly, "or they would not have left me here."

"Why are you here?" Asha asked. "What happened to you? Where are all the other males."

"The gods came, and they left. That's what they told me. And all the other males died. That's what they told me."

"You never saw them? The gods?"

"Nobody saw them," the Lemnian said. "But the gods spoke to them. That's what they told me."

"Who are 'they'?"

"The females."

Asha thought about that. The Lemnian leader had told her there were no males, but here was proof that she had been lying. And the other Lemnians, the females, had imprisoned this male for purposes that she was beginning to suspect.

"They did this to you?" she said. "The females? They keep you here?"

"Yes."

"And for what purpose?" She had to ask.

"To service them. What else?" The Lemnian looked unhappy and sicker. "At first," he said in a softer twitter, "I thought it would be a pleasure, all the females a male could desire. And then it became a duty I was required to perform for the Lemnian species. And then it became torture, and they kept after me day and night."

"I'm going to get you out of here," Asha said, moving toward the table once more.

"No," he said, raising his head as if in protest.

"Why?"

"They'll kill me," he said, and dropped his head back to the table.

Without warning, the door opened behind Asha. Lemnians rushed into the room to take her arms. They dragged her away.

The room was familiar. It was the office in which she had been interrogated, only now there were three older Lemnians, one seated and the other two standing on either side of her, like a panel of judges. The younger Lemnians who had brought her here remained standing behind her, one on each side, as if she had undergone a transformation from possible visitor to convicted prisoner. She could have disposed of them at any time, but that would get her only increased hostility and overwhelming force. The three behind the desk looked at her silently for a long, tense moment.

Finally the seated Lemnian spoke, using the rusty Galactic Standard she had used before. "You have lied to me. You are not an emissary of anything, except maybe the demons who seek to divert us from our service to the gods. Maybe you are a demon. Are you a demon?"

"It is you who have lied," Asha said. She had decided to reply in Galactic Standard. Her mastery of Lemnian twitter might yet be better concealed from these officials. "All the Lemnian males are not dead."

"That poor ineffective creature is scarcely a male. He has failed at the only thing he is good for."

"He does not impregnate the females?" Asha said.

"You know then?" The Lemnian official—now Asha thought she must be a leader, a mayor, a governor, or maybe someone at the national or world level—paused as if to reevaluate Asha's understanding. "He does not."

"He might perform better," Asha said, "if he were given food, rest, medical attention and—yes!—even freedom."

"We do not tell you how to treat your males," the Lemnian said, "if you have any. Do not try to tell us how to treat ours. Even if you come from beyond the sky, as you say."

"Have your males always been treated in this fashion? As impregnation creatures?"

"What else are they good for?"

"They are people, too," Asha said, "with feelings and minds and abilities that are equal to those of females."

"Myths."

"Well, this poor male needs some help. Bring in some other males."

"There are no others. The males all died."

"And why not this one?"

"He was found, cowering in a remote village," the Lemnian said. "He was fortunate to have lived past the day when the others expired, and he was happy to be brought here, alive, to serve his people."

Asha finally asked the question she had been wanting to ask since she first noted the absence of males and the Lemnian-in-charge had told her that the males were all dead. "And how did they die?"

"We killed them," the Lemnian said.

It was an unemotional statement that confirmed all the suspicions that had concerned Asha from the beginning. "Why?"

"They were lazy, unfaithful creatures," the Lemnian-in-charge said. "That's what the gods told us. And they told us to kill them."

"How?"

"How did we kill them?"

"How did the gods tell you?"

"In the customary way."

"And what is that?"

"By revelation," the Lemnian said.

"A message?"

"It was the kind of message gods send." The Lemnian turned to the Lemnian standing on her right and twittered, "This creature has no understanding and no use other than to ask meaningless questions." And she turned to the Lemnian standing on her left and twittered, "She is not from the gods. I think she is a demon. We should dispose of her like we did with the males."

Asha did not display any reaction to the judgment being discussed. That they did not know she understood their language might still be useful.

The two standing Lemnians made a movement with their heads that could have been approval. So, Asha thought, it was a sentence. "We will consider your words," the seated Lemnian said to Asha in Galactic Standard, but then twittered to her guards, "Take this person to the room with the male until we can dispose of her. And make certain that the door is guarded."

The two guards took Asha by the arms and turned her toward her fate.

CHAPTER THIRTEEN

Life in the red sphere was different with Asha gone. Despite the transcendent rationality, male competition between Riley and Tordor was more prevalent without the civilizing influence of a female, and Adithya was on edge about his responsibility for what was being reported by the medallion hanging about his neck.

Riley and Tordor argued about whose expedition had involved the greater peril, and when that ended without a conclusion, about whose investigation had obtained the most useful information. It was all pointless and served only to ease concerns on Riley's part about Asha's situation on Lemnia. Tordor's motivation was harder to read; maybe he was just being a Dorian.

"Asha is responding well to the Lemnian environment," the Pedia reported. "Conditions are not toxic as they were on Nepenthe or oppressive, as they were on Centaur."

"They were not oppressive on Centaur," Tordor said. "Only dangerous."

"Oppressive to a human," the Pedia said.

"Allow the Pedia to stay current," Adithya said.

"Conditions are optimal for human or humanoid existence," the Pedia said, "and so far there is no evidence of predators."

"What about alien invasion?" Riley said.

"Or of alien invasion," the Pedia concluded.

The Pedia fell silent, and in the absence of information on what was happening on the planet below, Riley and Tordor picked up their argument, only this time it concerned the red sphere. Tordor had never been as comfortable with the protean abilities of the ancient spaceship as Riley, who had lived with it for several long-cycles before Tordor had joined the crew. He also had the special relationship of the person who had discovered the artifact. Tordor continued to question the method by which the red sphere traveled between nexus points. It had no apparent means of propulsion, no engine, no expulsion of mass, no loss of matter, if the substance from which the red sphere was made could properly be considered matter, no diminishing or resupply of energy.

The Pedia broke into the conversation. "Lemnians have appeared. They have arrived on flying creatures, resembling oversized birds."

"Birds?" Tordor said. Heavy-planet aliens had no experience with flying creatures.

"Creatures with wings that travel through the air," Adithya said. "Quiet."

"Seven Lemnians have arrived. All of them apparently female. They have surrounded Asha. She speaks to them, although they do not understand her language. She does not resist as they take her to the avian transportation that brought them here. Asha is placed on a bird with a Lemnian behind. The group begins to fly."

"Is she in trouble?" Adithya asked. "Do we need to rescue her?"

"Her pulse rate has gone up. The experience is increasing the flow of adrenaline."

"I knew I should have gone with her," Adithya said.

"Asha is only reacting to the unfamiliar experience of open-air flying," Riley said. "And she is allowing the Lemnians to take her where she can obtain the information we need." He was not as unaffected by Asha's situation as he wanted Adithya to believe.

"As for the red sphere," he said, "I have my own theories about its abilities." Tordor knew that, because they had talked about it before, but it was good to distract Adithya from his concerns—and, he was aware, his own, being separated from Asha, except for his experience on Nepenthe, for the first time since they had been reunited on Earth.

The red sphere, he said, had been the means by which the creators of the Transcendental Machine had transported receiving devices, and the engineers who installed them, to worlds around the spiral arm that contained Earth and the Galactic Federation. Since ships like these were going to worlds that had no technological civilizations, they had to be self-sustaining, regenerative, resistant to widely different conditions. That is why this one survived a million long-cycles of neglect. Perhaps it also took representatives of local cultures back to the home planet for research or education.

"Or purposes less benign," Tordor said.

"Who knows?" Riley said. "But it would explain the ability of the red sphere to adapt itself to individual variations in physiology, diet, breathable air, and the rest."

Moreover, he went on, the creators of the Transcendental Machine were masters of particle entanglement and therefore, probably, masters of other particle sciences. One of those, from the available evidence, was the ability to transform space, which enabled them to create the system of nexus points by which the galaxy, or at least two of its spiral arms, became capable of practical interstellar travel. Who is to say, Riley asked, that particle theory and the ability to shape space did not also allow their ships to travel between nexus points without using macro devices of propulsion? As the evidence before them indicated that they did.

"In other words," Tordor said, "they used magic."

"Magic is what people call technology they don't understand," Riley said.

"If it is technology," Tordor said, "that is even more reason to return this ship to the Federation undamaged. It is technology the Federation may need to repel an alien invasion—if an alien invasion is what is happening."

"And a reason why we and the ship should not be destroyed when we return with the answer to that question," Riley said.

As for the energy supply, he went on, he had a theory that the red sphere absorbed energy from its environment when it was exposed to sources. Particularly to the radiation from suns. Its ability to respond and react at the cellular level suggested that it was also capable of absorbing and storing energy at the same level.

"Moreover," he said, "it may be that the fall of the roof of the building the dinosaurs constructed to house, and possibly confine, the red sphere may have saved it from extinction."

"The Lemnians with Asha have arrived at a metropolis," the Pedia said, "and she has been confined in a room."

"She has been imprisoned," Adithya said. "Take me down so I can help her."

"She doesn't need any help," Riley said. "Not yet anyway."

And the Pedia said, "She has said that she doesn't request any help at this time."

The absence of further reports about Asha's situation, except for routine statements that "Asha is eating" and "Asha is resting," allowed life to continue on the ship without further distraction but also without eliminating the tension that always existed when one of them was in a position beyond the group's immediate ability to help. It was a tension they had learned to live with.

Once Adithya raised a question: "Why are there only females?" And Riley responded. "I'm sure Asha has asked this, too."

Not too long afterward the Pedia reported that Asha had left the room in which the Lemnians had thought to restrain her and had entered another room, which contained a male Lemnian strapped to a table. The Lemnian told them that he was the last remaining male, saved to provide reproductive services. Asha had expressed some concern about the Lemnian's physical condition and offered to release him, but the Lemnian refused, for fear of being killed.

Then female Lemnians had entered and taken them back to the room where Asha had been questioned before.

"Asha is in trouble," Adithya said. "It's my responsibility to go help."

"She will ask for help when she needs it," Riley said. And, though he did not say it, Riley was not sure that Adithya was the one to offer it. Or, for that matter, any male.

The Pedia reported the interview, with all its troubling implications.

When Asha was taken back to the room with the imprisoned male, Adithya could be restrained no longer.

"Take me down," he said. "We can wait no longer."

"Why you?" Tordor asked.

"Because . . . ," Adithya said. "Because I should."

"I don't think the young person should go," Tordor said. "He has no experience."

"The only way to have experience," Riley said, "is to have it."

"I have the Pedia," Adithya said, holding the medallion out like a validation. "The Pedia that Asha gave me. I can always draw upon your experience."

"We'll need the medallion to keep in touch with Asha," Riley said. He held out his hand.

"We cannot let the young human go without assistance and without the means of asking for help," Tordor said.

"If you place me in contact with any metallic object," the Pedia said, "I can use that as a communication device, although only the medallions have the capacity to contain the full range of my abilities."

Adithya had an earring. He handed it over to Riley, extended the medallion, and the contact was made. Adithya restored the earring to its place and left the medallion in Riley's hands.

Riley took the red sphere down to the outskirts of the Lemnian city, unconcerned that it might be observed by Lemnians. From what he had learned about the Lemnian reason for killing their males, Adithya might need the benefit of a supernatural arrival.

"Always keep in mind," Riley said, "that these Lemnians killed all the males."

Riley watched Adithya press through the side of the red sphere onto the surface of Lemnia and disappear into the city.

Asha regarded the sacrificial male with compassion. She began unbuckling the straps that held him to the table, ignoring his protests. "Don't worry," she twittered at him. "I'll protect you."

She helped him sit up. The effort was almost too much for him, and he fell over when she let go. She pulled him upright again. "Stay there," she said before she went into the bathroom/kitchen for a cloth and some water. She returned to find him flat on the table once more. She bathed his face and body, noticing even more keenly how thin and weak he was. He was unresisting but agitated, turning his head from side to side. It was pitiful, Asha thought, that he had been reduced to this state of animal-like subjection to the Lemnian females. But perhaps it had always been that way on Lemnia, the males smaller and weaker than the females; or perhaps it was only this male who had been allowed to live because he was small and weak.

Asha got grain from the kitchen, mixed it with some water, and mashed it with an implement she found that was something like a spoon. She put a small portion of the gruel in the male's mouth. He let it dribble out the side. She wiped it away and tried again until he began to chew and then to swallow. After a few mouthfuls she paused and let him rest and then resumed until he had consumed half of what she had prepared. He rested again and then when she raised him to a sitting position, he stayed upright.

"Why do the females treat you so poorly?" she asked.

"Life is never easy," he said.

"Males are slaves?"

"That is the way it has always been."

"It just got worse," Asha said. "It is not just that the other males died. The females killed them all."

The information took a moment to register, and then the Lemnian began to tremble. Asha placed a hand on his shoulder to steady him. "Why?" he asked.

"It was a moment of madness," Asha said.

"The females are never mad," the Lemnian said. "They can be mean and they can be cruel, but they always have reasons."

"They say they received instructions from ancient gods," Asha said.

"There are no gods," the Lemnian said. "That's what you told me."

"If I am right," Asha said, "they only seem like gods. They are powerful creatures from places beyond the world you know. But the females were confused. They thought the ancient gods had returned and had commanded them to kill the males."

"From another world?" the Lemnian asked.

"You know about other worlds?"

"I have heard the females talk about ships that fly above the sky, about worlds like ours but different, with different kinds of people who live on them, even of organizations that govern the ways in which such worlds relate. But I have never seen such things. That is female business."

"Not any longer, apparently."

"You, too, are from another world."

"Yes, and I have come here to find out why your females have forgotten everything they have learned about their world and its place in the universe."

The Lemnian displayed the kind of helplessness that he had shown when Asha first encountered him. "If they have forgotten," he said, "there is no hope for Lemnia. Only death and extinction."

"That may be true," Asha said, "and my task may be to determine

CHAPTER FOURTEEN

how it happened and prevent it from happening to another world. But there is one possibility for Lemnian salvation."

"What?"

"You," Asha said.

"What can one worthless male do when the females have failed," the Lemnian said.

"I don't know," Asha said, "but I'll think of something. Meanwhile, rest and don't worry. This female hasn't failed yet."

The Lemnian lay back and closed his eyes. After a few moments he seemed to have gone to sleep. "All right," she said softly to the medallion, "what has been going on aboard the ship?"

"Adithya has left the ship and come to rescue you," the Pedia said.

"That's ridiculous!" Asha said. "Why didn't they stop him?"

"Tordor tried, but Adithya insisted and Riley allowed him to have his way. The young human is impatient, and it may be that Riley thought action might make him wiser."

Asha considered the long history of conflict between Latha's group of Anons and Earth's Pedia. "Now I will have to rescue Adithya as well."

"Adithya has entered the city. On the ship Riley and Tordor are disputing who is responsible for making your task more difficult and whether they should proceed with actions to rescue you both."

"They must do nothing yet," Asha said, and then, to herself, "Males!," before she recognized that she was committing the same mistake that she had ascribed to the female Lemnians.

Adithya had made his way only a couple of kilometers into the city when a squadron of Lemnians mounted on their oversized birds swooped down upon him, alerted, perhaps, by sightings of the ship's landing but unintimidated by its appearance. There were seven of them, as there had been for Asha. Perhaps that was the standard squad for a Lemnian patrol or perhaps they were the same seven with responsibilities for dealing with aliens, gods, and demons. They surrounded Adithya. He thought of resisting, but they were sturdy and seemed athletic, and perhaps they would take him where he needed to be. They twittered among themselves. Adithya imagined they were telling each other that another stranger had appeared on their world, like the previous one but with a different shape. Perhaps this visitor was a god coming from the sky, they might be telling each other, but more likely a demon.

"They are discussing whether to kill you now," his earring whispered, "or wait and kill you later."

They dragged Adithya to a bird and forced him to sit upon it until a Lemnian got on behind him and held him in place. She was strong. Adithya thought he could break away if necessary. He was slender but he had always been athletic, and life in Latha's commune had involved labor as well as games and exercise. Still, he needed to go where Asha had been imprisoned, and his captors might be his best means to join her.

He was heavier than Asha, and the bird he was riding had difficulty getting airborne. Soon he was experiencing the same terrifying passage through the sky as Asha, only over city roofs and spires rather than countryside. In a few minutes, however, his flock landed on a tall building, the bird he was on staggering and almost falling as it came to a stop. If everything had gone as he hoped, it was the same building to which Asha had been brought. The oversized cages on the circumference of the roof seemed similar to the ones the Pedia had described and the sliding door and the steps down to a corridor as well, though these circumstances might have been the same on a number of buildings they had passed over in their flight.

He was shoved into a room, perhaps the same room that Asha had occupied, though he could not detect any evidence that she had been here. The door slid shut behind him. He was alone in a prison on an alien world, and he didn't know what he should do next.

"Asha did not think this was a good idea," the Pedia said from his earring, its uninflected words echoing strangely in this unlikely location. "It seems she was right."

"For a thinking machine you are quick to make premature judgments." Adithya had reached a truce with the Pedia, recognizing its part in enabling the investigation of a possible alien invasion, but he could not entirely rid himself of the animosities of a lifetime.

"Even a thinking machine must evaluate the possibilities of success," the Pedia said. "But I am speaking for Asha. She has been informed that you are confined and instructs you to do nothing that will interfere with her plans."

"And what are those plans?"

"She has not confided in me."

"And until she does, I don't know what interference means, and I must take whatever action seems appropriate," Adithya said. "Open the door."

"That does not seem consistent—"

"We don't know what is consistent, do we? Open the door." Adithya put his ear against the door. The door clicked and slid aside. He found himself facing a Lemnian, who was not happy to see him. She twittered at him as she pushed him back and followed him into the room. The door slid shut. She stood in front of him, her back to the door as if challenging him to get through her, glaring at him, her arms folded across her chest.

"What did she say?" Adithya asked.

"It may be unwise—" the Pedia began softly.

The Lemnian's eyes focused on Adithya's ear, as if she had heard something.

"We need information," Adithya said. "It is a chance worth taking."

"She is saying that you are a demon like the other, but you are worse because you seem to be a male, though she would like to make sure of that."

"At least we know there is a connection with Asha," Adithya said. "Maybe she is nearby."

The Lemnian twittered at him and pointed at his ear.

"She wants to know what I am," the Pedia said.

"Tell her you are my translation device."

The earring twittered and fell silent. The Lemnian came forward, anger or distrust apparently put aside for the moment, and touched Adithya's ear before grasping it in her hand as if she were going to tear it away. Adithya put his hand on top of hers, holding it in place.

"Tell her," he said, "that the translation device is a part of me, and that it would be dangerous for both of us if it were removed."

A muffled twitter came from beneath the joined hands. Adithya felt

the Lemnian's hand loosen. He removed his hand. The Lemnian's hand
fell away, but Adithya noticed that it had lingered on his chest.

"Tell her," Adithya said, "that I am neither god nor demon. I am a
person, though of a different shape than persons here, and I have come
to her world from the sky to bring help to her people."

The earring twittered and the Lemnian responded. She had her
arms folded across her chest again and her twitters seemed more mea-
sured.

"She says," the Pedia reported, "that her people do not need any help.
Particularly they do not need help from someone who is not a god or a
demon but a male."

"Tell her," Adithya said, "that she is very attractive and that if the
world was fair she would have a large and attractive family and become
a leader among her people."

The male Lemnian stirred and sat up without Asha's help. He seemed
startled to see her nearby, where she had been waiting patiently for his
wakening, and then he seemed to remember what had happened. She
had a bowl of gruel in her hands and started to feed him again, but he
took the bowl and implement from her and began to feed himself.
Clearly he was feeling better.

When he had finished, Asha said, "Now you must tell me how to
send a message to the other Lemnians—the females."

"I do not know what you mean by a 'message,' " he said.

"Some communication other than speech," Asha said.

"I know of none."

"Some marks inscribed on a surface," Asha said. "Disposable, like
clothing, or permanent like glass or metal."

"Sometimes I have seen the females drawing," the Lemnian said, "but
this is female business."

"You have never learned to write?" Asha said. "Or to read?"

"I do not know what these words mean."

Asha tried another approach. "If the females received a message from
the ancient gods, how would it come?"

"There are no gods," the Lemnian said.

"But if there were," Asha persisted, "would the message come as a voice from the sky? Words from a box? Inscriptions on a surface?"

"There are no gods," the Lemnian said again.

Asha heard some noise on the other side of the door. It sounded like a scuffle. A moment later the door slid open and Adithya was thrust into the room by two sturdy Lemnians. He was bruised, but he was smiling. "Hello, Asha," he said.

The Lemnian guards glared at the three of them before they backed into the corridor and closed the door.

"Are you all right?" Asha asked. She was pleased to see him, but she did not want him to forget that he had ignored her instructions.

"I'm fine," Adithya said cheerfully. "I thought the Lemnians might throw me in with you if I made a disturbance, and that's how it worked out."

"At least," Asha admitted, "I don't have to find you."

"Nor I you," Adithya said.

Adithya was assuming an equality of judgment that Asha didn't think was justified by his age or experience, but she decided that was an issue for another time. "I have found out everything I'm going to discover in these circumstances," she said. "Apparently these Lemnians were invaded some long-cycles ago, by creatures they couldn't understand so they considered them gods, and the invaders told them to kill the males."

"An unusual tactic for invaders," Adithya said.

"But an efficient way to wipe out a people in a generation or two," Asha said. "Neat, too, without the need to dispose of bodies."

"But that doesn't seem to fit the other two situations we've seen," Adithya said.

"No," Asha admitted, "and for that reason I think the message, if it was a message, was misinterpreted, that the invaders affect the dominant species on each world in different ways, depending on the physiology and culture of each species, as if they are implanting mental toxins tailored to each situation. In some instances it is fatal. In others it wipes out higher mental functions. In still others, it eliminates cultural memories and implants instructions leading to species suicide."

"Unless that part is a mistake," Adithya said.

"Yes," Asha said.

"So you have learned something important," Adithya said. "And we can leave without feeling that the investigation has been a failure."

"That's true," Asha said and felt pleased that Adithya had felt the need to support her work here. It showed a level of maturity that she had not noticed in him before. "But I would like to do something to help the Lemnians and this particular Lemnian." She indicated the male who had been watching each of them in turn, as if he were trying to learn their language. "He's had a bad experience and a worse one awaits, and a better treatment might mean survival for the Lemnian species."

"How were you going to do that?"

"I was planning to leave a message for the Lemnians," Asha said. "As if it were from the gods who instructed them to kill the males. Telling them that they had done wrong and that they had to respect the male and treat him properly."

"Then why don't you?" Adithya asked.

"I don't know how," Asha said.

"As for that," Adithya said, "the Lemnians have a kind of electronic communication system, the sort of thing that is essential to a techno-logical civilization, though the Lemnians have forgotten how to main-tain it or that they built it in the first place. That's why they have reverted to using the birds for transportation. And that's how the so-called gods delivered their revelation. The Pedia ought to be able to figure it out."

"How do you know this?" Asha asked.

"There was a guard—" Adithya began.

"Never mind," Asha said. She turned to the Lemnian and twittered at him. "We're going to leave here in a few moments, but the females will treat you better if you insist upon your rights. Make them teach you and your male offspring to read and write. After all, you are going to be the father of your people."

She lifted the medallion from her chest. "Inform Riley where we are located, and that we will meet him on the roof in fifteen minutes," she said.

Adithya looked at her with respect. "Fifteen minutes?"

Asha did not reply. She placed the medallion against the door. When it clicked and slid open, she took the surprised guards by their throats and pulled them into the room, knocked aside their raised arms, and struck each across the side of the neck with the stiffened palm of her hands. The blows were as effective on Lemnians as they would have been on humans. They dropped unconscious to the floor. Asha pulled each one to the side of the table on which the male Lemnian was sitting, astonished and aghast.

"When they wake," Asha twittered at him, "tell them the gods have appointed you their savior, and good luck with everything. Now it's up to you."

She nodded to Adithya. They ran down the corridor, up the stairs, and out the sliding door onto the roof. Asha found a metal bar to prop the door shut, just as the red sphere descended, shattering some of the cages and freeing big, startled birds to flutter into the sky.

Asha and Adithya pushed their way into the ship. Riley took Asha in his arms. "Welcome back," he said, and then he gave his hand to Adithya. "You too."

"We've got to send a message to the Lemnians," Asha said.

"I know," Riley said.

"The Pedia told us," Tordor said. "It already has its means of transmission established."

Asha turned to Adithya. "But you shouldn't have come."

"As for that," Adithya said, "I have something else for you."

"What?"

"The message the ancient gods sent."

"How—" Asha begin.

"There was this guard—" Adithya began.

CHAPTER FIFTEEN

Once the ship was beyond the atmosphere of Lemnia and on its way out of the Lemnian solar system headed toward a nexus point, Asha filled in the details of her encounters with the militant Lemnian females, their disposal of the Lemnian males, who had always, it seemed, been regarded as mere sperm donors, and their discovery and mistreatment of a single male.

"What happened on Lemnia," Asha said, "was a consequence of the Lemnian evolutionary path and its subsequent cultural development. The attack by whatever is causing these widespread symptoms focused on a Lemnian weak point, by accident or intent, wiping out memories of recent Lemnian history, including its entry into space and contact with the Federation. The Lemnians reverted to earlier supernatural explanations, and a state of mind was created for a 'revelation,' whatever it was, to be interpreted as a command from ancient gods to kill all the males."

"The revelation seems to have been a message," Adithya said.

"And how do you know that?" Riley asked.

"A guard told me."

"Why would a guard tell you anything?" Tordor asked. "Or could, since you didn't speak or understand Lemnian."

"There are other ways to communicate," Adithya said. "And I had the Pedia to translate for me."

It was the first time he had said something good about the Pedia, and Asha considered that a sign of better working conditions. "You mean she found you attractive?"

"Is that so hard to believe?"

"You are a good-looking man," Asha said, "but you were a human and she was a Lemnian."

"But I am male," Adithya said, "and she was female."

"In the unlikely circumstance of cross-species attraction," Asha said, "there is the additional handicap on Lemnia of female dominance and male extermination."

"That only made our situation more intense," Adithya said. "Intensity sometimes enhances attraction."

"Attraction?" Asha said.

"You mean you had sexual relations with a Lemnian?" Riley said.

"As to that," Adithya said, "details are unnecessary. But surely, if something like that might have happened—an unlikely circumstance, as Asha has said—there would be no possibility of biological consequences."

"Cross-species fertilization?" Asha said.

"I am not saying that," Adithya said.

"Certainly not," Tordor said. "Unless the Lemnians need only stimulation for self-fertilizing processes."

"You're joking," Adithya said.

"On the contrary," Tordor said, "there are thousands, if not millions, of different species in the galaxy, and every one has a different evolutionary path with different evolutionary strategies for survival. In fact—"

"Anyway, she told me the 'revelation' that led to the massacre of the males," Adithya said. "Perhaps to impress me. Or to intimidate me. Of course I couldn't understand it. But the Pedia could."

"Well, what was it?" Riley asked.

"It seems to have been received electronically," the Pedia said, "although it may not have been transmitted—if that is the correct word—that way. The message that the Lemnian revealed to Adithya had many strange words and grammatical constructions, and it was in a language that is not only unfamiliar but of unique structure, not unlike the language of Earth's birds, rudimentary though that is."

"Enough of your excuses," Tordor said. "What was the message?"

"What I have is merely a jumble of what may be words," the Pedia said, "and it may take many cycles, perhaps long-cycles, to correlate these with previous discoveries from Nepenthe and Centaur—"

"Yes," Asha said. "We understand that conclusions are not possible, that all information is partial."

"Given all that," the Pedia said, "this is an approximation, in Galactic Standard, of what the Lemnian told Adithya."

A line of words appeared on the wall of the dining space that the red sphere had carved out for them:

> **Seeking US** are not ⬈□□○ our *the* it **SERVE** we *gulf* us ☺●● vast separates **THE** from *internal* purpose ♌◆◆ here suns **AND** searching purpose

The four of them stared at the line of words and symbols as if continued study could produce comprehension out of chaos.

"What do the symbols mean?" Riley asked.

"A place where the translation fails," the Pedia said. "Where more information is necessary."

"And the different sizes of letters and emphasis of words?" Asha asked.

"You are asking more than the medium can provide," the Pedia said. "This is, after all, a transcription of a verbal message in an alien language."

"There are no such symbols and emphases in Galactic Standard," Tordor said.

"Galactic Standard is limited in many ways," the Pedia said.

"And so is Earth's Pedia," Tordor said.

"And yet it is all we have," Asha said, "and I have confidence that, given time and further data, the Pedia can help us come up with an answer."

But she was not as confident as she sounded, and neither was Riley.

During the long journey to the nexus point, they had time to go over the cryptic message many times without getting any closer to its meaning. The Pedia was silent for long stretches, possibly devoting all of its resources to correlating the data from their explorations. It was capable of millions of calculations per second, but even the fastest calculations are no better than the information available.

At one point Riley said, "There's nothing in the message that would drive a Federation crew into maniacal homicide."

"Nor a civilized species into mindless prey," Tordor said.

"Or destroy an entire species," Riley added.

"And it doesn't contain any instructions to kill the males," Asha said.

"At least that we can understand," Adithya said.

"It is possible," Riley said, "that the Lemnian female didn't know the message. Never knew it. This kind of directive may go only to the top administrators, and the rest only follow orders."

"Why would she lie?" Adithya asked.

"People often pretend to be more important than they really are," Riley said. "And she knew you didn't understand her language. She could have made up anything, and you would have been just as impressed."

"And yet—" Asha began.

"And yet?" Riley said.

"And yet a message like this might well be shared as broadly as possible. If it really was received as a 'revelation' from ancient gods, it may have been distributed around the Lemnian world. Moreover, all the females had forgotten their recent history. Only the male somehow escaped, perhaps because he was considered too insignificant to be included, perhaps because he was hiding, perhaps because he was male."

"Which means," Tordor said, "that we have to assume that the absurd message is real."

"We can also make some other assumptions," Asha said. From the evidence so far, she pointed out, the response to the alien invasion, if that was what it was, was different in each situation they had investigated. Mass insanity, mass dying, mass virtual lobotomies, mass murder. Each seemed like an attack tailored for the vulnerability of each species. Or perhaps they were the same attack interpreted differently by each species, according to its own evolutionary history and culture.

"Either way," Riley said, "we are left with the question: What do the invaders want?"

"What all invaders want," Tordor said. "Destruction. Or conquest. Or both."

"But they conquer nothing," Adithya said. "They only destroy."

"Destruction is one kind of conquest," Tordor said. "Aliens are as difficult to categorize as people. Some kill just for the killing. Some kill to destroy the competition. Some have long lives and think in terms of hundreds or even thousands of long-cycles. They may be waiting to return after the worlds are depopulated."

"Some of our fiction writers have speculated that world wars or the poisoning of the environment or the climate are the work of aliens," Asha said.

"Nepenthe is already depopulated," Riley said. "But it is not a great place to live. Or breathe. Unless you were a Nepenthean."

"Centaur will be depopulated soon," Tordor said, "leaving only the tigers. And without centaurs to hunt, they too will die."

"And the Lemnians won't last longer than the life span of the youngest," Asha said, "unless my message convinces them that the gods have changed their minds, and they treat their lone male as their potential savior."

But even these discussions, circular as they were, could not survive the long, dull voyage between nexus points, the terrifying exhilaration of the passage through no-space, and then the seemingly endless journey from nexus point to the solar system toward which Tordor had directed them. It was a red dwarf sun, only one-third the size of Earth's sun and one-tenth as bright.

"Three-fourths of the galaxy's suns are red dwarfs," Tordor said, "and because they lose their energy resources so slowly, they will be around when all the larger, brighter suns have left the sequence and collapsed. Or exploded. They are the immortals of the galaxy, and their planets will still be thriving when the rest of the universe has gone dark."

The planets of the red dwarf had orbits close to their primary, like

children huddled near a feeble fire on a cold night. Closest was a onetime gas giant whose deep atmosphere had been blown away, even
by the weak solar winds, leaving a barren, rocky core that raced around
the red dwarf in a few cycles. But the next farther out was a blue world
that, though swift, took twenty-two cycles to orbit its sun. It was in the
Goldilocks zone where water was liquid, which for the red dwarf primary was only a few million kilometers from its muted glow. And that
meant the planet's oceans were liquid. Or ocean, to be accurate, because
the world was known in the Terran equivalent of Galactic Standard as
"Oceanus," Tordor told them. It was a water world, one ocean covering
the entire planet to a depth of hundreds of kilometers.

Aquatic life thrived in this environment. Although there were no continents or islands, seaweed floated to the surface and matted together
to form floating habitats, some lasting only a few cycles, others more
permanent, and on some of these creatures with gills crawled up, evolved
lungs, and sometimes returned to the ocean. Ocean life was layered,
with microscopic organisms at the top, converting sunlight and air into
carbon-based food and oxygen, feeding plankton and krill-like creatures,
who in turn fed fish and fishlike mammals; predators fed upon them,
and so on down to the depths, where armored and gelatinous life-forms
were nourished by the warmth and nutrients from hot springs.

Gradually the mammal-like creatures, who had evolved from creatures who climbed onto the floating islands and then, over the long, long
cycles, returned to the ocean, grew huge, and some developed the ability to dive deep for sustenance rather than straining the plankton and
krill from the top ocean layers. Inevitably they came into contact with
the denizens of the deep, particularly the great tentacled, large-brained
creatures who ruled the ocean floor. They would have great battles there.
Sometimes the mammal-like creatures would win and carry back to the
surface the tentacles of their prey and sometimes the tentacled creatures
would win, clutching their enemies in a death grip until they drowned.
And sometimes the mammal-like creatures would return, wounded and
scarred, to survive on the dead bodies that floated to the surface or to
return once more to the undersea struggle.

And so it went, generation after generation, with who knows what
epic narratives passed along in the sonorous messages the mammal-like

creatures transmitted across the upper regions of the ocean world. But
after hundreds of thousands, perhaps millions, of long-cycles the great-
brained mammal-like creatures shared a great thought. Throughout the
ocean's circumference and down to its deepest reaches, the song traveled until all the mammal-like creatures had heard it and participated,
and even the fishes and tentacled creatures understood that something
was happening that might change their watery world. One mammal-
like creature with better eyesight or greater curiosity than the others had
seen the sky and told his fellows about the sun that warmed them, the
clouds that covered the world, and the storms that troubled the ocean.
And another joined in the song to say that the creatures who lived in
the ocean need not be at the mercy of the sun or the clouds or the storm,
that minds could understand and shape a better environment for
everybody.

"In fact," Tordor said, "the mammal-like creatures discovered science."

"In Earth language," the Pedia said, "the word 'science' means 'knowledge.'"

And so they grew knowledgeable and passed along their knowledge
from generation to generation through the songs they sang, because they
had no means of recording their knowledge in any other way. They
became philosophers, thinking great thoughts but unable to translate
them into anything tangible. And so it went for more thousands of cycles, while the songs got longer and more complicated, until a new note
emerged. It suggested that something might be done to capture the
energy in the soft glow of the sun, to harness the storms, to tame the
waves, to make the minds of the ocean creatures the master of their
environment rather than the uncaring acts of nature. But, the thought
continued, the mammal-like creatures had no hands, no way to interact with their environment except through swimming and thought.

A response came: What about the tentacled creatures of the deep?
They had a way to manipulate objects. For some tens of long-cycles the
song continued until a new voice added a note: Let us find a way to talk
to the tentacled creatures. And the effort continued until finally a message was sent and received, and in a remarkable feat of reconciliation
the mammal-like creatures and the tentacled creatures formed a team

to shape their environments and understand their universe. Together they built a civilization on Oceanus.

"They could not construct a spaceship," Tordor said, "and it was only by cosmic accident that a Federation scientist discovered electronic signals from a place where no member of the Federation was known to exist, where, indeed, no star was visible, as most red dwarfs are not. A ship happened upon this dim system, discovered Oceanus, and reported to Federation Central. This was, of course, many thousands of long-cycles ago, but it has become legend. The philosophical musings of the mammal-like creatures have enriched the Federation's intellectual life, and the cleverness of the tentacled creatures has revolutionized many Federation practices. Only a few of the smaller tentacled creatures were ever taken into Federation space and returned, but the people of Oceanus became vital, though distant, contributors to Federation civilization.

"And now they too have gone silent."

"A remarkable story," Asha said. "I wonder how much of it is legend and how much is true."

"That is the problem with legends," Tordor said. "They always contain a kernel of truth, but it is not always possible to determine what kernel."

"But with a world like Oceanus and creatures like these," Riley said, "how are we ever going to find out what's happened?"

"We will have to be very ingenious," Tordor said, "and very brave. And perhaps a little reckless."

"We?" Riley said.

"It will take both of us," Tordor said.

CHAPTER SIXTEEN

The red sphere deposited Riley and Tordor on the largest of the floating islands. They wore protective red garments prepared for them by their ship out of its own substance through a process that they still did not understand. They argued about it in the long periods of travel, Tordor suspicious of the ship's mysterious and protean nature, Riley willing to trust the symbiotic relationship he had established since the discovery of the ship in the temple raised to house and contain it on the planet of the dinosaurs, Asha and the Pedia continuing to probe the nature of what Riley called "intelligent matter."

They would not be able to maintain the protection of their garments for the length of time it would take them to investigate the silence of Oceanus. The red film that enveloped them contained a reservoir of air in a bulge at the back, and it had a limited ability to process exhalations for breathable ingredients of oxygen and nitrogen, but this would not suffice for more than a cycle, particularly through moments of strenuous activity. The first thing Tordor did then, when he set hoof upon the matted surface of the island, was to push his trunk through the protective red surface of the suit and take a cautious breath.

After a few moments of suspense, he said, "The air is breathable. Humid and scented with the odors of the sea and the decay of vegetation, but not toxic. And the bacteria and viruses seem to be tolerable, or, at least, not above the level that our improved immune-responses cannot handle."

"I'll take your word for it," Riley said, although he thought that Tordor had experienced far more alien environments in his long Federation service, as well as far more immunizations against alien microbial threats. He stripped back the part of the red suit that covered his head. "We had better keep our suits on, however. They may be necessary if we have to explore the ocean itself. Or get exposed to it by accident."

The island was only a few kilometers across. Soil deposited by creatures and storms had bound the matted fibers together in what seemed like a solid surface, but it felt spongy under their feet. Insects swarmed up and small creatures scurried. It was, Riley thought as he swatted away some insects, an unpromising beginning.

"What now?" he said.

"Now we explore," Tordor said.

They tramped around the island and crossed its interior before they ended where they had begun, near the island's edge where it met the vast ocean that covered the entire planet. They had observed small animals looking something like fish out of water or crustaceans or habitat-building creatures that had fashioned small structures out of seaweed and mud who scurried into them when startled by such alien life-forms. But mostly what they encountered were insects that seemed to welcome them as new sources of food.

Riley swatted ineffectively at them. "Go away," he said. "You'll be sorry if you sample either of us." He turned to Tordor. "Okay. What next?"

"Now," Tordor said, "we wait for a great-brained mammal to contact us."

Riley looked out over the blue ocean, hoping to see the bulk of a huge sea creature breaking the surface; there was nothing but the ceaseless motion of wave and current and the barely perceptible rise and fall of the island under their feet. So it was for an entire Oceanus day, which was only half a dozen hours long and complicated by the swift rotation of the planet around its red dwarf primary, and an equally short night, which was brightened by the reflected light from planets much closer than in most solar systems so that they appeared as small round objects rather than pinpricks in the night sky.

"We can't just sit here fighting the bugs," Riley said.

"You are right, as always," Tordor said.

He knelt by the edge of the island, with the blue waves rolling gently toward his hoofs. He lowered himself to the surface, pushed his medallion through the yielding surface of his suit with his short trunk, and immersed it in the ocean. "What do you hear?" he asked.

From the ocean came garbled words. Tordor lifted the medallion. "We didn't understand that."

"Only the movement of the water," the Pedia said.

"Try again," Tordor said. "And this time listen to the sounds of the ocean. There are many sounds if you only listen for them. Sounds of life talking to life." He pushed the medallion back into the ocean and left it there for several minutes before he withdrew it once more.

"Well?" he asked.

"There are sounds there, muffled by the waves, but sounds that are more than the movement of water," the Pedia said. "I cannot discern anything that sounds like intelligence at work."

"We are too close to the island," Tordor said.

"And what does that mean?" Riley asked.

"One of us must go farther out, where the water is less disturbed."

"Yes?"

"And Dorians cannot swim," Tordor said. He looked at Riley.

"I am guessing that you mean me," Riley said. He was liking this expedition even less as it developed. He did not remind Tordor that he had grown up on Mars, where there was no body of water to swim in, and his only experience with deep water was when he had been dropped, by Jak's ship, into the lake near the city that had been reconstructed from the ruins of Las Vegas. But he stroked the red material that covered his body so that it closed over his head and slipped into the water, hoping that the suit would provide buoyancy. He tried not to think about the planet-spanning ocean that he had entered, a watery gulf that extended hundreds of kilometers beneath his body, a habitat for creatures large and small that might regard him as a heavenly gift for their consumption.

He struggled for a few minutes to keep his head above water and his feet and legs from sinking while his breath came too rapidly for his limited supply of air to sustain.

"Trust your body," the Pedia said. "Human minds are connected to glandular secretions of panic."

Riley focused on control of his adrenal gland's release of adrenaline, and his breathing slowed. His body stopped fighting the medium that threatened to swallow him, and he floated, rising and falling with the waves that moved under him. He thought of it as a bed that rocked him.

"Better," the Pedia said. "People are such fragile creatures. It is surprising that they survived long enough to create thinking machines."

"It is even more surprising," Riley said, "that they endured the machines' attitude of superiority for so long."

He had gotten the hang of it now and tried a few strokes of his arms that moved him through the water and then some swishes with his legs that propelled him faster. Soon he was meters away from the island and ready to try the sound detection once more. He pushed the medallion through the protective garment, turned over and let his face be submerged, trusting the red suit to protect him from the water, and thrust the medallion into the ocean. He let it remain for several minutes before he pulled it out and back into his suit again.

"Well?" he said.

"More sounds," the Pedia said. "Creatures swimming, creatures eating and being eaten, the almost inaudible photosynthetic processes of microscopic creatures turning sunlight into edible substance. The business of life wherever it arises."

"But what about the sounds we're trying to identify?" Riley said.

"Not yet," the Pedia said. "There are no sounds that contain communications. Perhaps farther out."

Riley took a few more strokes with his arms and kicks with his legs before he tried again. This time he allowed the medallion to remain immersed for nearly ten minutes.

When he brought it back into his suit once more, the Pedia said, "I heard the pattering of small swimming mammals as they seemed to be pursuing a school of fishlike creatures and maybe the distant mournful sound of a large swimming mammal. And the even more distant clamor of a great struggle."

"This doesn't seem to be working," Riley said.

"Such projects require time and patience," the Pedia said. "Living creatures have no patience."

"Living creatures are faced with the limitations of life spans," Riley said. "Unlike Pedias."

"Once more," the Pedia said.

Riley tried the process again. This time he gave it half an hour. Or he would have if he had not felt something beneath him, something that bumped his body out of the water for a moment and then allowed it to splash back. He gasped and was bumped again. He focused on his extremities, checking to see if any part of him was missing. Apparently not. The bumping had ceased. Perhaps whatever had checked him out was merely curious, not hungry. He raised his head from the water to look around. There was nothing to see in the water, nothing but ocean. In fact, he could no longer see the island.

At the moment he became aware of his isolation and the possibility that he didn't know where the island was, he was lifted into the air, up, up, and found himself on the back of a vast gray body, meters wide and many meters long, a leviathan, a mammal-like creature such as Tordor had described. And it was a creature engaged in a life-and-death struggle with a many-tentacled creature that had enveloped the leviathan's head and had closed what seemed to be the hole on the top of the head that enabled the mammal-like creature to breathe. And that hole, and the tentacle that closed it, was next to where Riley had been thrown to his knees.

Riley raised his head and found himself staring into the huge, enigmatic eyes of the tentacled creature staring back at him. It was like looking into a window into a different reality. Riley knew that was human response to the alien, but his instincts, controlled but not eliminated by transcendence, told him there was no compromise here between action and death. Instinct also led him to thrust the medallion still in his hand toward the closest tentacle, the one that was closing the leviathan's breathing hole. He felt the recoil of the shock that ran through the tentacle. The tentacle jerked away. The creature's eyes went blank for a moment. The leviathan seemed to take a deep breath and shook itself, flinging the tentacled creature high in the air, Riley along with it.

Riley splashed into the ocean. He righted himself and raised his head. The tentacled creature was meters away, but it was sinking into the waves created by the leviathan moving rapidly in the other direction. The tentacled creature, it seemed, could not swim or perhaps it was exhausted from its epic battle. Yet even in its going it seemed to be searching for Riley.

Riley swam the other way. He was swimming better now, propelled not by experience but by terror. As he went he pulled the medallion back into the suit.

"Slowly," the Pedia said. "Conserve your strength. You have a long way to go, and the attacking creature is no longer a danger."

"That's easy for you to say," Riley said between gasps for breath.

"I wasn't the one who got you into this fix."

"No, and I've got you to thank for getting me out," Riley said. And then, after another moment for breath, "I didn't know you had the ability to shock."

"I have many abilities you don't know about," the medallion said. "But you should focus on the task of getting back to the floating island. And you're off course. You need to be going more to your right."

"A sense of direction as well!" Riley said and devoted himself to swimming. It was something he thought he might enjoy if it was not always an act of desperation.

After a few minutes the Pedia said, "It wasn't electricity. It was an electronic command. And it seemed to work as well on alien creatures as on machines."

Half an hour later Riley pulled himself up on the edge of the floating island.

Tordor was standing a few meters away. As soon as Riley had stripped the hood of the protective garment from his head, Tordor said, "Welcome back. You took your time."

Riley looked at the Dorian with disdain. "I had a couple of interruptions."

"Useful, I hope."

"Well, I encountered one of your mammal-like creatures."

"And were you able to establish communication?"

"I was too busy saving its life," Riley said. "And my own."

"Really?" Tordor said skeptically. "In your first venture into the ocean?"

"And from the other half of the technological partnership you described."

"Results, so soon!"

"If you can call them that," Riley said. "I think the partnership has been dissolved."

"Ah," Tordor said.

"Permanently. The tentacled creature was intent on destroying the mammal-like creature and seemed to be succeeding."

"And you intervened?" Tordor's tone suggested that he did not believe anything that Riley had told him.

"It is true," the Pedia said. "It happened as Riley says."

"With the help of the Pedia," Riley said.

Tordor contemplated those statements for a moment before he twitched his trunk in a gesture that Riley had learned indicated assent or at least acceptance. "Then we have learned half of what we came here to discover. If the encounter that you describe is typical rather than an isolated incident, the partnership that created a technological era on Oceanus, as you say, has apparently been broken and the ancient enemies have returned to their previous positions of competition. But we still have no account of what has happened."

"As for that—" the Pedia began, when it broke off and then said, "There is a storm approaching. Apparently of considerable size and strength."

Riley looked toward the far side of the island. Indeed, dark clouds were climbing the sky.

The Pedia said, "You should be removed, but the crew of the ship doesn't know whether it can arrive in time."

Riley took another look at the clouds. They seemed to have moved closer in a very short period. "I think that's a good idea."

"This island might not survive a giant storm," Tordor said.

"If the storm is of hurricane proportions," the Pedia said, "the crew believes that it might not be able to get close enough for you to come aboard."

Riley felt the wind pick up and the island rise and fall under his feet, as if it were anticipating the end of its brief existence. And his.

CHAPTER SEVENTEEN

Inside the red sphere, Asha and Adithya felt the emptiness of the space-ship after Riley and Tordor had been left on the floating island. It was the first time they had been alone together since the time, on Earth, when Adithya had freed her from Latha's suffocating hospitality, and that encounter had far different dynamics: Adithya wanting to rid the commune of a disturbing influence and Asha wanting to get on with her mission of reconnecting with Riley. And now they were without the mediating influence of the Pedia. With the two medallions on Ocea-nus with Riley and Tordor, they had only the communication received by Adithya's earring.

"Riley and Tordor seem to be relatively secure," Asha said. "We should use this time to survey the rest of Oceanus."

Adithya nodded. "The Pedia agrees."

"You have made your peace with it?" Asha said.

"We have a truce," Adithya said. "I will not try to cripple or destroy it as long as it remains essential to our mission. And it will not try to control me as long as I serve a useful function."

"And you know this how?"

"Some things do not need saying," Adithya said. "Like the under-standing between you and Riley."

"That emerges out of strong mutual feelings of connection—what used to be called by the all-encompassing word 'love,'" Asha said.

"A similar reaction emerges from the strong mutual feeling of opposition, what used to be called 'hate,'" Adithya said. "I can no more shake the lifetime habits of distrust and antagonism than the Pedia can remove from its circuits its most basic directive, to serve and protect the people it finds necessary to suffocate.

"What may be more curious is Tordor's insistence that Riley accompany him."

"They are still working out their relationship," Asha said, "like two male animals circling each other over who is going to be the leader of the pack."

"They are supposed to be free of such juvenile impulses," Adithya said.

"Transcendence doesn't mean that you've had your biological impulses removed," Asha said, "only that you're aware of them and able to deal with them."

She had started the red sphere in its circuit of the planet. They were watching the viewscreen for any sign of variations in the surface of the ocean below but saw only the occasional floating island of matted seaweed similar to the one on which they had deposited Riley and Tordor, as well as occasional clouds and rainstorms. They noticed one more sizable meteorological disturbance over a section of ocean nearer the north polar region and another closer to the equator. They were moving rapidly but both were hundreds of kilometers from the floating island on which they had left Riley and Tordor.

"Riley and Tordor have found nothing of interest on the island," Adithya reported, "and now Tordor is using the medallion to listen for underwater communications."

"Another evidence of the Pedia's contribution to our investigation," Asha said.

"But without success," Adithya said. "Tordor is trying to convince Riley to swim out into the ocean."

"Riley can't swim," Asha said.

"Neither can Tordor. But Riley is entering the water. He seems to be struggling—"

"He'll drown!" Asha said.

"He is doing better," Adithya said. "Yes, the Pedia reports that he is swimming better."

Asha controlled the feelings of concern that welled up when Riley was in danger. He knew he was competing with Tordor for the position of dominant male, and he tried to keep that from coming into the open where it would have to be addressed. And in a way that would threaten their mission. But he also was willing to take risks that might lead to a discovery about the alien invasion, particularly if it was a discovery that Tordor could not make.

"Those mammal-like creatures that Tordor told us about," Asha said, "are a lot like the legendary animals that used to roam the seas of Earth. They were called 'whales,' I think."

"I have heard of them," Adithya said. "There were even reports before I was born of a sighting of what was believed to be one near what was left of the Antarctic."

"And the tentacled creatures. They are like the eight-limbed creatures called 'octopuses,'" Asha said. She was trying to distract herself, and perhaps Adithya, from thinking about what was going on in the ocean below.

"Or a similar creature called a 'squid,' the Pedia told me," Adithya said. "There still are a lot of those around, maybe more because the whales are gone."

"An example," Asha said, "of convergent evolution. Like Tordor's saber-toothed tigers."

"The Pedia reports that its sound-searching has not yet been successful, even farther out to sea," Adithya said. "But it is trying again."

Their talk subsided while they waited for more information from the watery world below. Some minutes later, Adithya said, "Riley has been attacked by some kind of sea creature!"

Asha thrust her fingers into the control window and felt the red sphere accelerate.

They had not traveled more than a few kilometers when Adithya reported that the sea creature was one of the whale-like mammals, and it hadn't attacked Riley; it had risen under him during its struggle with a tentacled creature. And then that Riley had saved the mammal and himself, with the aid of the Pedia, and was now swimming back toward the floating island. Asha tried to urge the red sphere to go faster, but its progress seemed frustratingly slow.

Adithya noticed that the storms they had seen earlier seemed to be strengthening. "It looks like they're joining," he said, "and being pushed in the direction of Tordor and Riley."

Even more reason to hurry, Asha told herself, but the red sphere, so swift in space where there were no visual references, seemed more limited when the ocean surface sped past underneath. And yet she knew that it was her urgency that made the difference.

"The storms are getting close to the island," Adithya said, "and the strength of their winds has picked up to superhurricane strength."

"Tell them," Asha said. "Tell them that a hurricane is coming."

"Riley has made it back," Adithya said. And then, "The Pedia has informed them about the storm."

"We've got to get them off the island before the storm hits," Asha said. But she knew they would be too late.

CHAPTER EIGHTEEN

The wind blowing across the island—blowing the island itself—picked up. That was the first sign. Then the wind quickened and the first gust of rain arrived. A savage blast of wind and rain followed, battering Riley and Tordor and causing Riley to stagger. The island began to resemble a raft being pushed by an unseen motor. Waves shoved it up and let it fall again, sometimes from tens of meters high, with a shuddering impact. Riley fell to the surface of the island and grabbed a handful of matted seaweed. He could feel the island beginning to break apart under his body. He looked to his left and shook the rain off the red film that covered his face and head. A few meters away Tordor was clinging to seaweed with his short, powerful trunk protruding from his own protective garment. Tordor was trying to say something, but the sound was muffled by the red film that enveloped all but his trunk, and the fury of the storm that was now upon them in full, irresistible force.

"Hang on, Tordor is saying," the medallion around his neck shouted at him. "The ship is on its way."

But it was not so easy to hang on, particularly as the island was bucking under him, rising up and thumping down like flotsam on a raging sea. Riley no longer had any doubt—the island was breaking apart. He grabbed for a more secure handhold and felt his fingers slip, looked to his side and, between sheets of rain, saw white water to his left and Tordor on the other side as the island broke into splintering rafts of debris. A moment later he felt the water swallow him. He fought his way to a tossing surface. In what he could see through the blinding rain, what was left of the island was getting farther away with each moment, and he was tossed about in the waves, sometimes submerged, sometimes riding a crest toward a sky that seemed as wet as the ocean itself.

"Tell them to hurry!" he shouted, and could not hear the Pedia's reply in the thunder of the sea.

Then he felt himself caught and lifted and had a moment of relief before he realized that what had caught him was a tentacle wrapped around his waist, and he was being dragged below the surface by a creature whose intentions were not rescue. A few meters down the force of the surface waves diminished and the thunderous roar of the storm and the churning sea. His protective garment kept out the ocean, but as he was pulled deeper the pressure began to build. He felt the red material begin to stiffen, as if it sensed the crisis ahead.

"If you can contact the ship," he shouted, "you should tell them we're in a hell of a fix."

"Communication is more difficult in these conditions," the Pedia said. "But perhaps if you could—"

"Yes," Riley said and thrust the medallion through the red film before it became too rigid. He pressed it toward his waist where the tentacle was wrapped. And nothing happened. He tried again. Again there was no response.

He pulled it back, and the red material snapped as it sealed itself against the pressure of the surrounding water. Only the medallion and his hand and arm were soaked.

"Apparently," the Pedia said, "this tentacled creature has felt my touch before and knows that it is not deadly."

"You think it is the same creature?"

"There is no other explanation," the Pedia said.

As Riley was dragged deeper and felt the protective red suit stiffen further in an effort to keep the depths from crushing him, he had a moment to think that the beast he had stopped from destroying the mammal-like creature must have been lurking near the floating island,

waiting for a chance to get revenge. Or, if that was too complex a motivation, for a chance to get a meal when its previous prey had been taken
from it. And then he thought about the great ocean that covered the
entire planet to a depth of unknown kilometers and how long the intelligent matter that made up the protective garment the red sphere had
prepared for him would be able to keep him from being destroyed, either
by the ocean depths or the beast that was pulling him down into them,
or, less dramatically, using up his last reserve of air.

The descent seemed endless, and only the red suit kept him from being drowned before he was squashed. The substance hardened until he
felt like a larva inside a cocoon, unable to move his arms and legs or to
turn his head to see more than straight ahead. He was not complain-
ing. It was that or instant death, and there was nothing to see except
darkening water. And while he was still alive, there was hope.

"Is there any answer from the ship?" he asked.

"It too is caught up in the storm," the Pedia said, "and it is having
difficulty touching down on the island without destroying it."

"And of reaching us?"

"The atmospheric disturbance has created problems for location as
well."

"So we can't hope for rescue any time soon."

"So it seems," the Pedia said. "But we must act as if help was imminent."

The truth of that was evident but hard to believe. So Riley focused
on the water surging past his face and the occasional fishlike creature
that swam past, until, at last, deep in the water's dark depths, he saw
a glimmer of light.

The glow from the ocean floor revealed the tops of slender projections
that grew into taller spires like stalagmites and then slowly seemed transformed before his eyes into fairy towers illuminated by fluorescence
coating their exteriors, and he realized that these were not natural for-
mations but structures created by creatures like the one that was dragging him down into them. In spite of the probability of imminent death,
Riley wondered about the imagination and ingenuity of the creatures

buried beneath kilometers of ocean designing and constructing this magical city on the ocean floor. As he was drawn down between towering buildings, getting glimpses only as his protective cocoon was twisted by the movements of his captor through the water, slower now at these depths, Riley could see small, armored fish with fluorescent skins or lamp-like growths emerging from their foreheads swimming among the towers. He noticed that the luminescence came from organisms coating the exterior. He also could see that the structures were broken and weathered in places, as if they were ruins rather than functioning buildings.

Farther down he got glimpses of a different kind of glow from what seemed to be a fracture in the ocean floor and wavering distortions in the light that might have been water heated by lava beds under the ocean bed, surrounded by long strands of ocean life halfway between animal and vegetable. And then smaller tentacled creatures that came close as if to inspect what had been drawn into their midst and larger creatures who seemed as if they would contest his captor for its prey.

One of the largest of the tentacled creatures attacked, its flailing arms revealing something like suckers on the underside. Riley had a moment of hope that the creature who held him might release its grasp to fight off the attacker and he would surge toward the surface, but it struck back with its other tentacles and the attacker, battered, retreated. His captor, triumphant, dragged him farther down, away from all the rest, until they had reached an open space between buildings, like a plaza or a park if this had been a city in the open air. The creature settled down as if this was its lair or its private castle and held Riley up in front of its domed head and giant, staring eyes. It was, Riley realized, the same look he had seen in the eyes of the beast that had nearly killed the mammal-like creature, and perhaps the Pedia was right—maybe this was the same one and it recognized him as the source of its frustration.

The creature raised another tentacle and wrapped it around Riley's body, tugging at the red suit that protected him from both beast and ocean depth. The garment did not give way. The creature twisted the tentacle that held him in a direction opposite to the one it had placed above, as if it were trying to wring him apart. The red suit yielded for a moment, as if surprised, and then resisted. The creature paused to reconsider its options and then raised Riley above its head and slammed him to the ocean floor. It shook Riley's entire body. The suit continued to protect him, but another blow like this, he thought dazedly, might be his last.

At that moment a large, dark shape cut off the luminescence from the surrounding structures. Something huge and amorphous descended upon the two of them, Riley and the tentacled monster that held him, and a giant, gray object, square and blunt like a battering ram, struck the creature holding him, knocking it several meters away. The tentacle that held him did not release, but the gray object, Riley now realized through the waves of vertigo that rippled through him, was the forehead of one of the mammal-like creatures. Perhaps, he thought, it was the creature whose life he had saved, and as his vision cleared he saw scars on the creature's head where some tentacled creature's suckers would have been attached. Yes, perhaps it was the same one, or simply another swimming behemoth out for its own meal.

And then the mammal-like creature struck again, this time opening a giant mouth to bite down on a raised tentacle. In shock, the monster released its grip, and Riley shot free, like a cork released to shoot toward the surface. Riley had a moment to regret that he would not be able to observe the ending of the undersea battle between monstrous rivals before he focused on his own problems.

He had no experience with diving or ocean depths, but he remembered from somewhere in his past reading, suddenly available to him from a memory that no longer forgot anything, that sudden decompression could cause deadly bubbles to form in his veins, and he sent his thoughts into his body, willing his veins and arteries to compress. As if in response, the suit that had protected him in the depths squeezed tighter around his body. It could not slow his ascent, but with Riley's mastery of his own body they might minimize the damage. He felt his heart slow in response, but it did not stop.

And then he popped to the surface and into the air above it before he fell back, still living, aching but not fatally damaged. The sky was still gray and rain still fell, but the wind had quieted and so had the waves. He rested for a moment on the rolling surface, feeling the debris from the destruction of the island brushing against his body and wondering what had happened to Tordor when the red sphere descended beside him, a hand reached out and pulled him through into the ship. It was Adithya's hand, and he grasped it as if it were the hand of salvation.

Riley stood dripping inside the red sphere. He wiped his hand down his head and side, and the red garment that had saved his life fell in a shapeless heap to the floor and was absorbed into the substance of the ship like rain into dry soil. "Where's Asha?" he asked. His voice was husky, but it was a surprise to him that he could talk at all.

"At the controls," Adithya said. "Where her skills were even greater than her concerns."

"And what about Tordor?"

"Here," Tordor said, stepping out of the tunnel that led to the dining facility the red sphere had carved out for them.

"He was able to hold on to a patch of the floating island, and we got him back as we were searching for you," Adithya said.

Riley felt the force of acceleration as the ship lifted itself out of the gravitational grasp of Oceanus. Asha appeared from the tunnel that led to what they had come to call the control room. There was no way of knowing what the people who had built the red sphere had used it for, if it had even existed.

She put her arms around Riley and hugged him hard. It was nothing like the squeeze of the red suit, but it had the same life-sustaining effect. "Welcome back, partner," Asha said. "We thought we had lost you this time."

"Me, too," Riley said, and hugged Asha.

"Are you all right?" she asked.

"Except for some aching joints and the feeling that spiders are running across my skin," Riley said. "But that will pass."

"It is unfortunate that we have to leave Oceanus without discovering any answers to why it has fallen silent," Tordor said.

"This place is too dangerous for explorers who aren't prepared or equipped for a waterworld like this," Asha said. "The storms, the lack of solid land, the ocean and its invisible dangers—"

"The protective garments the ship provides are remarkably versatile,"

Riley said. "They saved my life. Helped by the mammal-like creature that attacked my captor."

"Maybe," Adithya said, "we have reached the limits of our ability to find the answers we are seeking."

"Without discovering what has silenced world after world?" Riley asked.

"We have to measure our resources against the challenges," Adithya said. "We may be too few and too poorly equipped to accomplish what we set out to do."

"Adithya may be right," Tordor said. "It might be wiser to return to Federation Central for reinforcements and resupply. This intelligent matter that chance and Riley's resourcefulness supplied us with is versatile, even miraculous, but it doesn't substitute for targeted technology or personnel replacements in the case of loss. Our failure here is proof of that."

"If we return," Asha said, "we will face the regulations you cited requiring automatic annihilation, and, if we avoid that, a delay of longcycles in mounting another expedition to discover the details of what may be an alien invasion. And, in the interim, more worlds will have fallen to attacks that we still don't understand."

"We could alert the Federation to the general nature of the threat so that it could prepare," Tordor said.

"Against what?" Riley asked. "We still don't know much more about the nature of the danger than we knew at the beginning."

"And we may be able to learn little more," Adithya said. "We should face the limits of our abilities."

"As for that," Riley said, "we have learned that the danger is primarily mental. Every species has had its minds affected, and we transcendentals may be the best equipped to cope with the kinds of attacks that drove a Federation crew into homicidal frenzy. And we learned on Oceanus that the ancient partnership between the mammal-like creatures and tentacled creatures has returned to its even older competition between behemoth and beast. And I saw the civilization that their partnership had created on the ocean floor, one that was beginning to fall apart like their truce. We seem to be getting closer to the source of what is happening, and even if we have no additional clues to meaning—"

on on Riley's chest said, "I have informa-

.

the long, low, mournful sound of the Ocea-

world
pro-
ation
t was
s was
im-
and
enges
ransi-
scen-
t life
order.
l-like
king
that
hat it
they
song
crea-

CHAPTER NINETEEN

Travel to the nexus point that would take them to their next silen[t] was tedious, as always, and Asha could not help wondering about t[he] gress of the alien invasion over the long-cycles that their invest[igation] had consumed. But they also had been gone long-cycles from w[hat was] happening at Federation Central. Not far from her everyday thoug[hts was] what was happening to their plans for transforming the varied a[nd im]perfect species that made up the Federation into more reasonab[le,] reasoning creatures: transcendents capable of coping with the cha[llenges] a still enigmatic universe could spring upon them. Completing the [transi]tion from the struggle for survival to the drive to understand. Tr[anscen]dence was one more tool in the unending struggle between intellig[ence] and brute matter, between plan and accident, between order and d[isorder.]

The Pedia repeated the long, mournful song of the great mamm[al] creatures of Oceanus until it filled their dreams as well as their w[aking] moments. When at last Adithya complained and Tordor agree[d that] they could not endure the sounds any longer, the Pedia told them [it] could continue its analysis without their participation, but tha[t they] possessed what he did not. They had organs for hearing and th[is] was meant to be heard. It could model the song digitally, but onl[y crea]tures with ears could respond to it as sound and melody.

"Unfortunately," Asha said, "we interpret its meaning according to our own physical equipment, which varies from species to species and by individual differences and experiences. The song sounds sad, but that may be a human response to a unique set of tones and melodies, and those may be determined not by choice but by the sound-producing organs of the singers. And even to identify it as a song suggests the impulse to place phenomena in recognizable categories."

"But there is a suggestion here," Riley said, "that this is a narrative—a story of epic struggle against great difficulties that ends with defeat and sorrow."

"I agree with that," Adithya said.

"If we are not bestowing on it our own values," Tordor said. "Or at least the values of humans. Dorians have no songs."

"Like Pedias," the Pedia said, although its typical matter-of-fact communication did not suggest whether this was a compliment or a criticism. "My analysis, however, suggests that Riley and Adithya are correct. There is a message here, a long message, what Riley has called a narrative, and I am beginning to understand it."

"And what is it you understand?" Adithya asked.

"The song—and it is a song according to the comparisons in my data bank—has a long opening passage of similar frequencies punctuated by moments of sharp increases in frequency, which I interpret to be a saga of long stretches of ordinary existence interrupted by conflicts, perhaps with the tentacled creatures, perhaps with giant storms such as the one we experienced, perhaps both," the Pedia said.

"That sounds no better than guesses we might make," Tordor said.

"But based on analysis," the Pedia said. "And then, in the middle, a calm passage where the frequencies are low and undisturbed, which I interpret as the time in Oceanus history when the mammal-like creatures convinced the tentacled creatures to join in creating a technological civilization—a Golden Age, if that human term can be applied to this alien world."

"Hardly appropriate to this watery planet," Adithya said.

"Go on," Asha said.

"Toward the end of the song, a slow rise in frequency brings it to a steady, higher state, which may be the period when the Federation discovers the Oceanus civilization and the mammal-like creatures in-corporate in their saga a more complete understanding of the universe that they had only philosophized about," the Pedia said.

"That sounds reasonable," Tordor said.

"And then, at the end of that long passage that represents a kind of grand finale to a symphony of origins, struggle, mastery, and compre-hension comes a sudden clash of frequencies leading to a sharp spike that ascends higher than anything before."

"The arrival of the alien invaders," Riley said.

"A conclusion that I have also reached," the Pedia said. "And those sharp notes are followed by a return to the theme of the opening pas-sage. And that is where it ends."

"Poetry," Tordor said. It was clear that he did not think much of poetry.

"And yet that is what epics are," Asha said. "An attempt to express the inexpressible, to imply in a few well-chosen phrases of language or song the indescribable complexities of life and experience."

"That gets us nowhere," Tordor said.

"A beginning," Riley said.

"Exactly so," the Pedia said. "What remains is a closer analysis of the penultimate phrase of the song, that moment when, if my evaluation is correct, the aliens arrived and changed everything. By comparing that passage with the information we have gained from our earlier discover-ies, I may be able to determine what it was that attacked the tentacled creatures, though perhaps not the mammal-like creatures, or not to the same extent."

"May, if, perhaps—all those indefinite qualifiers. We have something more solid and certain to consider," Tordor said.

"And what is that?" Asha said.

"The next world we have to investigate," Tordor said. "The deep at-mosphere world of Aerie."

"Aerie is a strange name for a planet," Adithya said.

"You will come to understand why that name is appropriate," Tor-dor said. "Of course this is how the Federation refers to this world, just as it refers to my planet as Dor, which means the world of rolling plains where Dorians live, and to Earth as Asylum, the world of troubled humans. They are not the names the native species give their worlds, which all are variations of 'the world.'"

Aerie, Tordor went on, was a world much more like Earth than like Dor. It was the same weight as Earth but sixty percent larger, which meant that it had a thick, gaseous atmosphere. Its sun was also a dim red dwarf but this one was ninety percent as large as Earth's sun. Aerie orbited in the favorable zone where the temperature was neither too hot nor too cold for water to remain liquid. Aerie was, of course, much closer to its primary than Earth. Still it might have evolved into a world much like Earth except that it either accumulated a larger, deeper atmosphere during its formative period, or retained much more of it, perhaps because the solar wind emitted by its sun was minimal. As a consequence the atmosphere of Aerie is thick and deep, much more like that of a gas giant than that of a normal rocky world, but without the gas giant's mixture of toxic gases.

The creatures that evolved in this unusual environment, Tordor said, were shaped by it, as all creatures are. That is the wisdom of the scientists who have studied these matters on a multitude of Federation worlds. On Aerie, microscopic materials in the sea clumped together into larger aggregates that developed into creatures who evolved into larger creatures that crawled out onto the land. The pressure of the atmosphere that benefited vegetation made life less advantageous for animal existence, and storms were even more common on Aerie than on Oceanus. Living in the air, however, was far easier, and land creatures of all kinds evolved wings while microscopic plants and plankton-type creatures were blown into the sky and some evolved into permanent residents, able to transform the sun's energy more available at that altitude into carbon-based compounds. The upper atmosphere of Aerie, where the air was not as thick and storms were less common, became filled with flying creatures and the basic foods they lived upon.

One of those flying creatures, challenged for its existence by competition, adopted tools and developed the brains necessary to handle them. With this advantage, they secured their evolutionary future and the understanding of their world that led to the development of self-awareness and the curiosities that go along with it. At first they built structures on the tops of their highest mountains, where they had once constructed their nests, and then they constructed platforms that soared at high altitudes, even higher than the mountains, to absorb the feeble energy of their sun and to harvest the vegetation and plankton. Slowly the platforms were transformed, bit by bit, into habitats and then into cities, and the winged creatures created an aerial civilization above the clouds where they could see the other planets of their system, which were much closer than those around a more radiant star, and then, beyond their own system, the other stars.

Finally they converted some of their harvesters into ships to explore their planetary neighbors and finding none of them capable of nourishing life they converted their spaceships into interstellar transports that, over the long, long cycles, eventually made contact with the Federation. The Aerieans became an apprentice member.

"All your descriptions of these worlds have the same inspirational theme," Riley said.

"The story of galactic civilizations share a common basic narrative," Tordor said. "They either succeed in fulfilling their potential, or they fail and their stories are never told. The story of successful species is written by evolution."

"Joining the Federation isn't my concept of nirvana," Riley said.

"Nirvana?"

"A state of final bliss, the perfect condition that ends all striving."

"A condition without striving is no better than death," Tordor said. "Joining the Federation is reaching the stage in a species' existence when everything becomes possible. Even discovering a Transcendental Machine."

"Which you and the Federation tried to stop," Riley said.

"To my regret. But if you want inspiration, think of the Aerians who set out to explore the stars. Winged creatures accustomed to soaring free in the air in a way that a Dorian like me could not even imagine. Confined to a metal prison for generations, sacrificing their flight, even amputating their wings, so that they might eventually reach their goal—that is inspiring."

"And so," Asha said, "we may discover that all their sacrifices were for nothing."

They had time to consider all of those possibilities while the red sphere sped, at what seemed like a crawl, toward the nexus point that would take them to their next appointed task. Riley and Tordor quarreled about Tordor's theory of galactic history and the meaning of what they had discovered so far, Asha tried to find a middle position that they all could agree upon. Even Adithya found moments of disagreement with Tordor about the Federation Pedias and their control over the bureaucracy that had developed to use their services and had their roles reversed without knowing it. And the Pedia reported periodically about its progress in analyzing the various bits of evidence their previous explorations had produced.

Then, when their waiting seemed as if it would never end, they reached a nexus point and experienced once more the out-of-this-world experience of un-space and emerged once more into the material universe. They faced another long passage from that place to the solar system of the planet Aerie. They had not yet reached halfway to their destination when the Pedia announced a breakthrough in its analysis of the Oceanus creatures' song.

"By comparing it with other communications from the worlds we have already investigated," the Pedia said, "I have managed to produce a partial translation of the critical portion of the mammal-like creatures' narrative."

"By critical," Riley said, "you mean that portion of sharp disturbance."

"That is correct," the Pedia said. "The rest is far easier to translate, and I could give you a rendering of the mammal-like creatures' epic story from simple beginnings to complex conclusions, and transitions from easy satisfactions punctuated by life-and-death struggles to the more complicated pleasures of critical discovery and self-analysis—"

"Enough of that," Tordor said.

"We can hear the mammal-like creatures' epic later," Asha said. "There will be time enough of that before we reach Aerie. What's the important part?"

Words, or what might be words, appeared on the wall of the red sphere:

Serve dying ⚹□▫○ protect energies bodies ♋•• nourished heat plentiful ♌◆◆ used up youthful

"This is nonsense," Tordor said.

"It is no more than we got from the Centaurs," Adithya said. "If your solution in that case had any merit."

"Similar but different," Asha said.

"Asha is correct," the Pedia said. "Cryptic still, to be sure, but a further step toward a more complete understanding."

"How so?" Adithya said.

"There are words still to be deciphered," the Pedia said, "but by comparing what we have discovered with other possible messages, we are another step closer to an answer."

And so the long next journey went, with time enough, as Asha had promised, to listen to the mammal-like creatures' epic, with its brief, cryptic and tragic interlude, not once but many times when there was nothing else to relieve the monotony of travel through featureless space. It was, indeed, a gripping narrative of life and love and death, of striving and success or failure and defeat, of evolution at work, finally guided by thinking creatures to a better end, and then final destruction. And particularly gripping when accompanied by the music of the mammal-like creatures, the sad low tones, the triumphant glimpses of other worlds and the concepts that bred philosophical musings, and the discovery of other solar systems and other intelligent creatures in them.

Asha, at least, listened, and Riley sometimes listened, but Adithya almost never and Tordor not at all. The Pedia, however, never tired of repeating itself, which was, to some, its least companionable trait and to others the computer characteristic that made it indispensable.

Finally, however, the system of the Aeriean sun swam into what served them as a viewscreen in the control room of the red sphere. It was a compact system, clustered close to its stingy primary: a clutter of ice and stone materials in an outer belt with an occasional dwarf planet accu-

"And so," Asha said, "we may discover that all their sacrifices were for nothing."

They had time to consider all of those possibilities while the red sphere sped, at what seemed like a crawl, toward the nexus point that would take them to their next appointed task. Riley and Tordor quarreled about Tordor's theory of galactic history and the meaning of what they had discovered so far, Asha tried to find a middle position that they all could agree upon. Even Adithya found moments of disagreement with Tordor about the Federation Pedias and their control over the bureaucracy that had developed to use their services and had their roles reversed without knowing it. And the Pedia reported periodically about its progress in analyzing the various bits of evidence their previous explorations had produced.

Then, when their waiting seemed as if it would never end, they reached a nexus point and experienced once more the out-of-this-world experience of un-space and emerged once more into the material universe. They faced another long passage from that place to the solar system of the planet Aerie. They had not yet reached halfway to their destination when the Pedia announced a breakthrough in its analysis of the Oceanus creatures' song.

"By comparing it with other communications from the worlds we have already investigated," the Pedia said, "I have managed to produce a partial translation of the critical portion of the mammal-like creatures' narrative."

"By critical," Riley said, "you mean that portion of sharp disturbance."

"That is correct," the Pedia said. "The rest is far easier to translate, and I could give you a rendering of the mammal-like creatures' epic story from simple beginnings to complex conclusions, and transitions from easy satisfactions punctuated by life-and-death struggles to the more complicated pleasures of critical discovery and self-analysis—"

"Enough of that," Tordor said.

"We can hear the mammal-like creatures' epic later," Asha said. "There will be time enough of that before we reach Aerie. What's the important part?"

self-awareness and the curiosities that go along with it. At first they built structures on the tops of their highest mountains, where they had once constructed their nests, and then they constructed platforms that soared at high altitudes, even higher than the mountains, to absorb the feeble energy of their sun and to harvest the vegetation and plankton. Slowly the platforms were transformed, bit by bit, into habitats and then into cities, and the winged creatures created an aerial civilization above the clouds where they could see the other planets of their system, which were much closer than those around a more radiant star, and then, beyond their own system, the other stars.

Finally they converted some of their harvesters into ships to explore their planetary neighbors and finding none of them capable of nourishing life they converted their spaceships into interstellar transports that, over the long, long cycles, eventually made contact with the Federation. The Aerieans became an apprentice member.

"All your descriptions of these worlds have the same inspirational theme," Riley said.

"The story of galactic civilizations share a common basic narrative," Tordor said. "They either succeed in fulfilling their potential, or they fail and their stories are never told. The story of successful species is written by evolution."

"Joining the Federation isn't my concept of nirvana," Riley said.

"Nirvana?"

"A state of final bliss, the perfect condition that ends all striving."

"A condition without striving is no better than death," Tordor said. "Joining the Federation is reaching the stage in a species' existence when everything becomes possible. Even discovering a Transcendental Machine."

"Which you and the Federation tried to stop," Riley said.

"To my regret. But if you want inspiration, think of the Aerians who set out to explore the stars. Winged creatures accustomed to soaring free in the air in a way that a Dorian like me could not even imagine. Confined to a metal prison for generations, sacrificing their flight, even amputating their wings, so that they might eventually reach their goal—that is inspiring."

as it refers to my planet as Dor, which means the world of rolling plains where Dorians live, and to Earth as Asylum, the world of troubled humans. They are not the names the native species give their worlds, which all are variations of 'the world.'"

Aerie, Tordor went on, was a world much more like Earth than like Dor. It was the same weight as Earth but sixty percent larger, which meant that it had a thick, gaseous atmosphere. Its sun was also a dim red dwarf but this one was ninety percent as large as Earth's sun. Aerie orbited in the favorable zone where the temperature was neither too hot nor too cold for water to remain liquid. Aerie was, of course, much closer to its primary than Earth. Still it might have evolved into a world much like Earth except that it either accumulated a larger, deeper atmosphere during its formative period, or retained much more of it, perhaps because the solar wind emitted by its sun was minimal. As a consequence the atmosphere of Aerie is thick and deep, much more like that of a gas giant than that of a normal rocky world, but without the gas giant's mixture of toxic gases.

The creatures that evolved in this unusual environment, Tordor said, were shaped by it, as all creatures are. That is the wisdom of the scientists who have studied these matters on a multitude of Federation worlds. On Aerie, microscopic materials in the sea clumped together into larger aggregates that developed into creatures who evolved into larger creatures that crawled out onto the land. The pressure of the atmosphere that benefited vegetation made life less advantageous for animal existence, and storms were even more common on Aerie than on Oceanus. Living in the air, however, was far easier, and land creatures of all kinds evolved wings while microscopic plants and plankton-type creatures were blown into the sky and some evolved into permanent residents, able to transform the sun's energy more available at that altitude into carbon-based compounds. The upper atmosphere of Aerie, where the air was not as thick and storms were less common, became filled with flying creatures and the basic foods they lived upon.

One of those flying creatures, challenged for its existence by competition, adopted tools and developed the brains necessary to handle them. With this advantage, they secured their evolutionary future and the understanding of their world that led to the development of discovers the Oceanus civilization and the mammal-like creatures incorporate in their saga a more complete understanding of the universe that they had only philosophized about," the Pedia said.

"That sounds reasonable," Tordor said.

"And then, at the end of that long passage that represents a kind of grand finale to a symphony of origins, struggle, mastery, and comprehension comes a sudden clash of frequencies leading to a sharp spike that ascends higher than anything before."

"The arrival of the alien invaders," Riley said.

"A conclusion that I have also reached," the Pedia said. "And those sharp notes are followed by a return to the theme of the opening passage. And that is where it ends."

"Poetry," Tordor said. It was clear that he did not think much of poetry.

"And yet that is what epics are," Asha said. "An attempt to express the inexpressible, to imply in a few well-chosen phrases of language or song the indescribable complexities of life and experience."

"That gets us nowhere," Tordor said.

"A beginning," Riley said.

"Exactly so," the Pedia said. "What remains is a closer analysis of the penultimate phrase of the song, that moment when, if my evaluation is correct, the aliens arrived and changed everything. By comparing that passage with the information we have gained from our earlier discoveries, I may be able to determine what it was that attacked the tentacled creatures, though perhaps not the mammal-like creatures, or not to the same extent."

"May, if, perhaps—all those indefinite qualifiers. We have something more solid and certain to consider," Tordor said.

"And what is that?" Asha said.

"The next world we have to investigate," Tordor said. "The deep atmosphere world of Aerie."

"Aerie is a strange name for a planet," Adithya said.

"You will come to understand why that name is appropriate," Tordor said. "Of course this is how the Federation refers to this world, just

"Unfortunately," Asha said, "we interpret its meaning according to our own physical equipment, which varies from species to species and by individual differences and experiences. The song sounds sad, but that may be a human response to a unique set of tones and melodies, and those may be determined not by choice but by the sound-producing organs of the singers. And even to identify it as a song suggests the impulse to place phenomena in recognizable categories."

"But there is a suggestion here," Riley said, "that this is a narrative—a story of epic struggle against great difficulties that ends with defeat and sorrow."

"I agree with that," Adithya said.

"If we are not bestowing on it our own values," Tordor said. "Or at least the values of humans. Dorians have no songs."

"Like Pedias," the Pedia said, although its typical matter-of-fact communication did not suggest whether this was a compliment or a criticism. "My analysis, however, suggests that Riley and Adithya are correct. There is a message here, a long message, what Riley has called a narrative, and I am beginning to understand it."

"And what is it you understand?" Adithya asked.

"The song—and it is a song according to the comparisons in my data bank—has a long opening passage of similar frequencies punctuated by moments of sharp increases in frequency, which I interpret to be a saga of long stretches of ordinary existence interrupted by conflicts, perhaps with the tentacled creatures, perhaps with giant storms such as the one we experienced, perhaps both," the Pedia said.

"That sounds no better than guesses we might make," Tordor said.

"But based on analysis," the Pedia said. "And then, in the middle, a calm passage where the frequencies are low and undisturbed, which I interpret as the time in Oceanus history when the mammal-like creatures convinced the tentacled creatures to join in creating a technological civilization—a Golden Age, if that human term can be applied to this alien world."

"Hardly appropriate to this watery planet," Adithya said.

"Go on," Asha said.

"Toward the end of the song, a slow rise in frequency brings it to a steady, higher state, which may be the period when the Federation

CHAPTER NINETEEN

Travel to the nexus point that would take them to their next silent world was tedious, as always, and Asha could not help wondering about the progress of the alien invasion over the long-cycles that their investigation had consumed. But they also had been gone long-cycles from what was happening at Federation Central. Not far from her everyday thoughts was what was happening to their plans for transforming the varied and imperfect species that made up the Federation into more reasonable and reasoning creatures: transcendents capable of coping with the challenges a still enigmatic universe could spring upon them. Completing the transition from the struggle for survival to the drive to understand. Transcendence was one more tool in the unending struggle between intelligent life and brute matter, between plan and accident, between order and disorder.

The Pedia repeated the long, mournful song of the great mammal-like creatures of Oceanus until it filled their dreams as well as their waking moments. When at last Adithya complained and Tordor agreed that they could not endure the sounds any longer, the Pedia told them that it could continue its analysis without their participation, but that they possessed what he did not. They had organs for hearing and the song was meant to be heard. It could model the song digitally, but only creatures with ears could respond to it as sound and melody.

"As for that," the medallion on Riley's chest said, "I have information that may help."

"What kind?" Asha asked.

From the medallion came the long, low, mournful sound of the Oceanus behemoth's song.

mulating enough mass to acquire a satellite or two, a couple of gas giants with assorted moons, and then Aerie, in the privileged zone, followed by a couple of lesser worlds too close even to their cool red dwarf sun to support life.

Aerie looked different from any world that Riley and Asha had ever seen, and even Tordor found it unusual. It was completely shrouded in clouds. Riley compared it to Venus, whose early history turned it into a furnace world wrapped in embalming-fluid-like gases, or Jupiter's envelope of gases kept in constant motion by hurricane-like winds that lasted for hundreds of long-cycles. But here, above the clouds of Aerie, were bluer layers of atmosphere with occasional brown patches.

"What are those?" Asha asked.

"Swarms of floating plankton, I think," Tordor replied.

And then, as they got closer, they saw the first of the floating cities, riding above the clouds, glittering in the reddish rays of the dwarf sun. They were not close enough to discern individual structures nor any signs of life, and the Pedia reported that it could not detect any electronic emissions that might indicate a thriving technological civilization, so it was unlikely that their approach had been noticed.

"It raises the question, however, of how we are going to put investigators on those cities," Asha said. "We can't land this ship on one, even if that were possible, without being observed and avoided—or attacked."

"You need wings," Tordor said.

"Wings?" Asha said.

"We are going among winged creatures," Tordor said. "Aerieans are humanoids with wings."

"Where are we going to get wings?" Asha said.

"You will have to get them from the place you and Riley get everything," Tordor said. "From this intelligent-matter vessel you get along with so well."

"Even if we could do that," Riley said, "the kind of wings the red sphere might provide would be nothing like the wings the Aerieans have."

"At least," Asha said, "it would get us to one of their cities."

"Us?" Riley said.

"Adithya and me," Asha said. "We might have some chance of going unnoticed, at least for a while. You're too sturdy for wings, and Tordor—well, Tordor could never pass for a flyer or a humanoid either."

"But you've never flown," Riley said.

"Nor have you. Anyway, as you did in the waters of Oceanus, we can learn."

"Are you all right with this, Adithya?" Tordor asked.

"I can do it if Asha can," Adithya said. "Humans have always wanted to fly."

It was something less than that. And something more. Getting the red sphere's cooperation was difficult. Its matter may have been intelligent, but it wasn't omniscient, and producing a workable wing was not an easy concept to transmit, as Asha had learned to do, concentrating her thoughts on a realizable outcome. But she did not know how a wing functioned, and even with the Pedia's help with design the red sphere required several attempts before it produced something that looked like wings. They emerged from a garment that covered Asha from head to foot.

From there it was a matter of nerve and practice. The nerve came into play when the ship descended into Aerie's upper atmosphere—though still as dense as Earth's at sea level—and Asha had to push her way through the ship's permeable skin and launch herself into the air and feel herself falling helplessly into the shrouded world below. The first few attempts were nearly catastrophic as Asha tried to get the wings beating and plummeted through the sky before she was caught by the red sphere descending beneath her.

"There once were birds that did not flap their wings," the Pedia said. "They spent long hours in the air soaring on wind currents and rising columns of air while they searched the land or the sea for prey."

On the fourth attempt Asha spread her wings and soared. It was exhilarating, and she felt a curious empathy with the Aerieans that she had never met and the freedom their wings gave them to inhabit their vast, atmospheric domain. Adithya required even fewer attempts to adopt Asha's technique and soon they were performing intricate soaring maneuvers before being swallowed up again by the red sphere.

Until at last the time arrived for them to trust their newfound ability without the safety net of the ship. It was time to land on an Aerie city.

CHAPTER TWENTY

It wasn't much of a jail cell as cells go, but it was good enough. On Federation Central there were no criminals. It wasn't that people on Federation Central were always law-abiding—or rather "regulation-abiding," because there were no laws; in a consensus society, there is only proper behavior and improper—people who did not behave properly were returned to their home worlds, where they faced whatever fate their local customs dictated, or they were transported to prison planets, or, if neither of those options was available and the breach of behavior was egregious, exposed to the cold embrace of airless space.

What distinguished Jer's cell then was its lack of qualities that distinguish most cells, except one. The walls were bare rock. The cell had been carved out of the barren planet on which the world-girdling structure that housed Federation Central had been built. Probably it had started as temporary housing for workers before they were able to put up more suitable quarters on the surface. After that it was used as a store-room. Both uses meant it was very old, though it had been outfitted with a few modern conveniences, a pallet made for a larger creature than Jer, a bench, a spigot for water, and a disposer for bodily waste. But it did have one distinctive feature of cells—sturdy metal bars at one end of the space that Jer now had occupied for six months, or half a long-cycle

as the Federation counted it—and a barred metal door with a lock operated remotely, probably only by command of the Pedia that controlled all the rest of Federation Central.

Jer had no visitors for the entire period of her imprisonment until
the very end. The only interruptions of her solitude were the arrival of
food containers under the barred door, delivered by a mindless scuttling
machine, controlled by the Pedia. The machine also retrieved the used
containers when Jer pushed them back under the bars, but it had no
capacity for speech. That didn't matter at first. The food was adequate—
level-two cuisine, she judged, rather than the basic level-one gruel—
but that didn't matter either. She was not interested in food, or speech
either, at least not for the first two months. She spent a great deal of
time thinking about what she could have done differently and what the
future held for her and the transcendents and the Federation, and, indeed, all sapient life in the galaxy. She had allowed her impatience at
the stubborn refusal of Federation scientists to apply their special skills
to the test at hand, and she had tried a dramatic shortcut to understanding. And it had landed her here, without results and without an explanation for the breach of conduct that had imprisoned her and left her
helpless to affect events.

Which had led her finally to address the machine that delivered her
meals. "Look," she said in Galactic Standard. She could have used
human, but she wanted to approach whoever or whatever was listening
as a citizen of the Federation rather than a supplicant human. "I know
you're monitoring me, as you monitor everything else on this miserable
excuse for a world you call Federation Central. I want you to know that
I'm monitoring you, too, and all the other Pedias who have brought this
galaxy to its sorry condition."

The mindless serving machine went about its mindless task without
a pause, but then she didn't expect a response. A month later she tried
again. "I want you to know that I represent no threat to you or to the
people you serve and protect. Instead I bring hope for a better and more
secure future for the Federation through new and improved technologies."

The silence of Jer's cell, which only her recent attempts to communicate had broken, engulfed her once more. A month later she made her

final attempt, again addressing the lowly food-delivery servomechanism. It was, at least, something to talk to, and she was getting a little concerned about her mental state. "The Federation is facing its greatest test since Federation Central was constructed, bigger than all the wars that have threatened its consensus, including the human/Federation war. Aliens with unknown powers and intentions have invaded, and the ordinary measures that have helped the Federation survive its earlier tests no longer seem to work. You need help."

The food-serving machine stopped in the act of sliding a food container under the barred door. "What help can a miserable, disgraced, and imprisoned human provide to a Federation that has endured and prevailed for two hundred thousand long-cycles?" it said. It had speech capabilities after all.

"The inventiveness and resourcefulness and stubborn survival characteristics of a species that has always struggled against great odds including taking on the entire Federation and fighting it to a standstill," Jer said.

"Aided by dissident elements of the Federation," the scuttling machine said, "and betrayal from within."

"Only after humans had demonstrated their ability to survive Federation attacks," Jer said. "And that elements of the Federation were willing to breach Federation consensus suggests a basic issue with Federation consensus and a growing problem with Federation creativity and tolerance for change."

"All of which has been restored," the machine said. It resumed inserting the food container under the bars, like a period at the end of a concluding sentence.

"And yet worlds at the edge of the Federation have fallen silent," Jer said. "And only a few humans and a Dorian are attempting to find out why. All official Federation attempts have failed."

The scuttling machine had returned to its previous silent state, and the Pedia, through it, was saying nothing more. That lasted another month, while Jer's attempts to restore communication went unanswered.

She had resigned herself to more silent contemplation and had nearly completed a mental reconstruction of the Jak Machine with new fixtures capable of accepting the shapes and sizes of all Federation citizens, a simplification of its control system, and an expansion of its capabilities, when the serving machine spoke again. "The purpose of imprisonment has been served," the machine said. "You are free to go." The lock on the barred door clicked, and the door came ajar.

"But my purpose has not," Jer said and pulled the door shut.

A few cycles later a Dorian showed up at the barred door. Jer recognized him—he was clearly male—the lead scientist who had rejected her explanations for what the Jak Machine could do and had consigned her to this cell. The cell door clicked as he approached. He pulled the door open, entered the cell, closed the door behind him, and rocked back solidly facing Jer, his trunk twitching slowly. He clearly was not concerned that Jer might attack him, and he was probably right. He outweighed her by several hundred pounds of muscle developed to withstand a world several gravities greater than Earth's, much less a satellite orbiting Ganymede, or Earth's moon, where she had spent most of her life. And his trunk looked deadly. Jer remained seated on the bench that had grown so familiar that it seemed almost an extension of her body.

When he spoke, his voice did not display the same disdainful, skeptical dismissal that it had during the presentation of the Jak Machine. Instead his tone seemed moderated, perhaps even approaching the tone that he might have used speaking to another Dorian. "My name is Baldor. I was the chief scientist at your demonstration."

"I know who you are," Jer said.

"I hope you have had time to consider your offense," he said.

"I certainly have had the time if I knew what the offense was," Jer said.

Baldor looked at Jer impassively, like all Dorians, but his trunk was twitching. Jer thought that, given time, she might be able to judge a Dorian's state of mind from the movement of its trunk. "You committed one of the gravest breaches of behavior against the Federation. The Federation has few regulations, because Federation citizens understand proper behavior. But the Federation cannot overlook behavior that threatens its existence."

"And how can a scientific experiment that does not explode or contaminate threaten Federation existence?" Jer said.

Baldor looked at Jer as if her question was not worthy of an answer, and then he said, "The most important aspect of Federation consensus government is the secret location of Federation Central. It provides status, authority, and protection from unstable individuals or regimes. Civil servants are brought here in Federation Central ships. The only citizens allowed to know Federation Central's coordinates are representatives of its constituent worlds to the Federation Council."

"And yet Asha knew them, because she was imprisoned here, and now so do Riley and Adithya," Jer said.

"All of whom would have been imprisoned, like you," Baldor said, "had it not been for Tordor's intervention. It was a serious breach of Federation protocol and one that Tordor might well have been called to answer for if he had not left Federation Central."

"And yet the council did nothing," Jer said.

"It was a sad day for the Federation—and for Dor. Tordor will have a difficult time explaining his failure of judgment."

"If he returns," Jer said.

"There is that," Baldor said.

"And if he returns," Jer said, "it will be as the hero of the Federation, the champion who ventures far from the tribe, defeats the enemy, and returns with great things for his people."

"You speak in mythical terms."

"Humans have come to understand the way in which legends describe and inform our behavior. But they do not explain my imprisonment," Jer said.

"When you appeared in our midst," Baldor said, "you raised the specter of the total loss of our most precious protection against attack, against insurrection, against betrayal: our location. What would happen if anyone, anywhere, could be transported to Federation Central? How could we control that? It would overturn everything about Federation life that is essential to our existence, to our very image of ourselves."

"Surely that is a matter of logistics," Jer said. "As long as no Jak Machine is allowed on Federation Central itself, it carries no threat of violating your seclusion. But your concern concedes the capabilities of the Jak Machine to transport people—and information."

"I concede that."

"And you have no doubt done your own tests."

"We have," Baldor said.

"Including transportation of living creatures," Jer said.

"Of course. First animals. And then people."

"And the results were as I demonstrated."

"Even more."

"In what way?"

Baldor's trunk twitched even more dramatically. "We instructed the Xiforan to transport itself. It was hesitant, but as the junior scientist it had no choice. After two initial failures to manipulate the controls, the Xiforan succeeded in bringing itself to push the buttons initiating the process and appeared in our Federation Central laboratory, blinking and dazed but alive. But different."

"How?"

"The Xiforan who appeared in our midst was not the wily, paranoid creature we all knew. Instead he had become as stable, as trustworthy, and, though I do not say this happily, as intelligent as any Dorian."

Jer looked at Baldor as expressionlessly as the Dorian. "And this concerns you in what way?"

"Clearly your Machine has capabilities that you did not disclose, capabilities that threaten the Federation even more than the loss of its secret location," Baldor said.

"To have Xifora as capable as Dorians?" Jer asked.

"That is unsettling," Baldor said, "and to have unsuspecting future users of this device emerging changed from the transportation experience would be even more unsettling. No governing body, even one as benign as the Federation, could survive a citizenry constantly changing in basic nature and capabilities."

"It might take a different kind of Federation," Jer said, "but it would be a better one, better equipped to cope with unpredictable events such as the emergence of humans into the galaxy or the rumors of a Transcendental Machine, or, more pressing now, an alien invasion."

"That would mean a sacrifice of Federation stability and ten thousand long-cycles of peace—marred only by the Federation/human war—for an uncertain future."

"The future is always going to be uncertain," Jer said. "But this is not all about the experience of your junior scientist, is it?"

The Dorian was silent for a long moment. "Of course not," he said at last. "As a scientist I had to try the experiment myself, and my transformation was as unsettling as that of the Xifor."

"You did not welcome the transformation?"

"Dorians see themselves as the end product of self-inflicted change," Baldor said. "They do not entertain the possibility of improvement."

"And yet there is room for improvement."

"All the customary ways in which Federation citizens adjust to each other will change," Baldor said.

"What you mean is that you will have to relinquish the subtle distinctions you make between species," Jer said, "with the Dorians at the top of the leadership scale and the Xifora at the bottom. Or perhaps humans have replaced the Xifora."

"All social connections are woven into the tapestry of civilization."

"Change will come only gradually," Jer said, "as people use the Machine and emerge changed, perfected. It will happen to individuals, not species, until finally, perhaps, a critical mass is achieved and everything will be transformed."

"How many will use the Machine when they learn that it destroys them at one end while it re-creates what is, essentially, a different person at the other?" Baldor said. "A scientist like myself might volunteer out of scientific curiosity, but the average bureaucrat?"

"Don't tell them," Jer said.

"Would that be fair?"

"Is life fair? Is evolution fair? There is a force toward improvement that shapes us all, that increases our ability to survive in a universe that seems bent on our destruction. One of the expressions of that is the tools we invent to extend our capabilities, like the Pedias that have been created to free us from the everyday necessities that keep us from imagining what understandings and accomplishments we are capable of. This is just the next step in evolution. Technology has shaped us all while we weren't paying attention, and we are now being shaped by the cultural forces we have unleashed rather than by arbitrary changes in the natural environment."

"Fine words," Baldor said. "Difficult application."

"And yet essential to the survival of sapience in the galaxy."

"There is one matter I have not addressed."

"What?"

"Your father."

"Jak? The creator of the Jak Machine?"

"He is a most difficult human."

"He is indeed," Jer said. "But he is not my father; he is the person from whom I was cloned."

"That explains a great deal," Baldor said.

"But how did you meet him?"

"Your machine worked at planetary distances," Baldor said, "but I had to investigate its range. Could it work at interstellar distances? The inventor of the device had to have one, and I finally discovered the means to connect with it. Your father—your clone father—was not pleased to see me."

"But he did not throw you into a cell," Jer said.

"He wanted to," Baldor said, "but he resisted the impulse."

"You see? He has changed. A few long-cycles ago he would not have resisted."

"We worked out an agreement."

"And all this conversation has been a mere ratification?" Jer said.

"You are part of it. Including your freedom."

"I could have walked out of here at any time," Jer said. She made a low growling sound deep in her throat, and the lock clicked in the door. The door came ajar. "But my business here was not finished. Now perhaps it is."

"I do not like the avenue we are taking," Baldor said. His trunk twitched spasmodically before he got it under control. "It goes against all the instincts of Dorians, all the traditions of the Federation, all the culture of civilized beings."

"The universe has great challenges yet to throw at intelligent beings," Jer said. "The societies that we have developed, the technologies we have created, the explosion of stars, the appetites of black holes, the dying of galaxies, the death of matter itself. This alien invasion is only the latest. We can hope that Riley and Asha and Tordor, yes, and Adithya, too, will be able to stop it, or, at least, to return with information about what it is and what must be done."

"And what if they fail? What if they don't return?"

"Then we—you and I and all the other people who go through the Jak Machine and come out the other end better than they went in— will have to be the ones that save the galaxy."

CHAPTER TWENTY-ONE

Asha and Adithya decided to land at night, when the approach of their ship would be less likely to be observed and even the descent of winged aliens into their city might go unnoticed. If the Aerieans were like most birds, they would roost at night. The Pedia noted, however, that some birds foraged at night, and flying rodents flew mostly at night.

"Let us hope," Asha said, "that they are not like the owls or bats of human legend."

The Aerie city that looked fragile in the viewscreen looked no more substantial from a few kilometers away as Asha and Adithya swooped above its crystal towers and nest-like amphitheaters looking like they had been spun from glass. They would look even more spectacular in daylight, Asha thought, when the sun's rays, feeble as they were, would turn the structures into frozen flame.

The amphitheaters seemed to be covered by discarded garments. Asha thought they must be sleeping Aerieans, enfolded in their wings, and she motioned Adithya toward an open space between spires that seemed deserted. As they got closer, it looked like a plaza or gathering place, perhaps where the Aerieans strolled before they took flight, ate whatever their diet involved in cafés that bordered the open space, and perhaps listened to ethereal sounds appropriate to a people who soared the skies.

They had not practiced landings, and managing their wings in a way that allowed them to come down gently on their feet led only to a tumbling arrival.

Asha stood up. "That was rough," she said.

"I could have done a better job," the medallion on her chest said.

Adithya rubbed his elbow. "It's a good thing we had the red sphere's garment to protect us, or our expedition might have been over before it started."

Asha shrugged her shoulders, and the wings were absorbed into the garment. She stuck her nose through the portion that covered her head and took a cautious breath. "You are right," she said to the Pedia. "The air seems breathable, though a bit chill. It has an odd odor, like all alien worlds, but this one smells like—I don't know—animal refuse." She stripped the garment from her head and body and stowed the material, now reduced to not much more than a flimsy handful, into a pocket of her coveralls. She might not look like an Aeriean, but with a red garment and ruby wings she would stand out even more.

When she turned, Adithya had done the same. "What now?" he asked.

"We check out the neighborhood. Before the citizens wake up."

The open space, the plaza, was paved with a smooth, transparent substance that looked and felt like glass. The plaza was dark, lighted only by Aerie's modestly sized moon, but Asha could see that smaller structures surrounded and defined the area. Like the pavement, their fronts were transparent though colored, each one a different shade as if to identify their purpose or to set them apart from their neighbors.

Asha and Adithya walked across the plaza, its surface slick under their feet. They felt bouncy as if the surface was resilient, and Asha thought for a moment that it might be the response of a floating city but realized that it was the psychological response to a gravity less than she expected. Closer to the buildings, Asha noticed scattered trash, some of it looking like feathers, some the detritus of a city without good street cleaning. She pointed it out to Adithya. The plaza was not as fairylike as it seemed. She picked up and examined one of the feathers. It was short, perhaps a tail feather, and it resembled the feathers she had seen in museums on Earth. Perhaps feathers were evolution's answer to the question of flight.

The first structure they reached had a glassy front with a yellow tinge. Asha could not see an entrance, though the unbroken front was scratched in places, as if some impatient customer had tried to enter when the place was closed. Asha could see only a meter or two into the dark interior. She saw benches and perhaps a counter or a line of tables. Maybe it was a restaurant.

Next to it was a slightly wider storefront with its transparent surface stained purple. The surface, however, was not intact. A darker space in the front indicated an entrance that had not been closed or was broken. The shape was not rectangular but rounded and larger above than below, as if to provide entrance to something broader toward the top. Asha stepped inside and let her vision adjust. To her left were shelves that seemed to support glassy jars and bottles. To her right, what looked like brushes and combs hung on the wall as if glued there by some mutual attraction. Between were a series of low, rectangular tables. This was a place where Aerieans got groomed or treated for whatever aches or ailments afflicted flyers, she thought.

Asha stepped back and wondered why the entrance had not been repaired. Maybe it was a public service always open and free to whoever needed it.

The next front had a blue tinge, and it, too, was unbroken. Through its tinted transparency Asha could see what seemed like garments hanging, without means of support, from glassy walls. Perhaps flying creatures needed protection from the cold of the upper atmosphere or simply liked to dress up.

Asha realized that she was seeing farther into the interior of this front than the others, and as she turned back toward the plaza, Adithya tapped her on the shoulder and indicated the far wall. The first light of a rising sun had turned the structures into mirrors reflecting their radiance across the space between.

Now Asha could see the entire plaza area, entirely enclosed by low buildings without avenues for entering or leaving. Appropriate for a population that flew, she thought, but not for visitors like her and Adithya. They would have trouble leaving.

"Let's conceal ourselves and see what happens," she said.

"Where?" Adithya looked around the plaza. In a city built of glass there was no place to hide.

"Here," Asha said. She motioned to the storefront they had just passed, and led the way through the entrance into the structure and hoped nobody would need grooming or massage first thing in the morning.

Confronting the Aerieans could not be avoided, but perhaps they could learn a little more before that critical first encounter occurred.

The first Aerieans arrived shortly after daybreak. Asha imagined them rousing in their spun-glass nests, spreading their wings in the warming sun, shouting into the morning sky with the joy of living, bursting into the air. They came, slanting down from the sky, one at first, then two and three, swooping, tumbling, coming to a standing stop in the middle of the plaza with a majestic forward spread of wings. And then the slow gathering of the wings around the body like a living cloak and a slow turning to inspect surroundings.

The scene seemed like a performance from some celestial ballet, almost mind-shattering in its beauty and grace. Asha took a deep breath and wondered what it would be like to own the sky, to wheel and cavort without concern for gravity or normal constraints of movement, so unlike the clumsy soaring that she and Adithya had done on red sphere wings that seemed now like an ugly parody.

She watched, hidden in the darkness of the grooming facility, as they approached singly and in small groups, and was surprised to see them not as splendid as they seemed in the air. Their feathers seemed dusty and with patches on them that might be mold. She could not see their bodies, folded as they were within their wings, but their faces were not angelic; they were ugly, with prominent eye ridges, sharp, beak-like noses, and slits for mouths that occasionally parted to reveal carnivore-like teeth.

Adithya nudged her as if to call her attention to the Aerieans' appearance.

"Beautiful or repulsive," Asha whispered. "It shouldn't matter." She realized that she was trying to convince herself.

"And yet this is what humans do," the Pedia said.

"Sh-h-h!" Asha whispered, and felt a cold hand on her arm.

She turned. Behind her were three Aerieans, with the ugly faces she had seen on the plaza though softer, somehow, as if gentled by time and experience. They had slender bodies covered and concealed by short, brown feathers. But, most important, they had no wings. Was it possible that there was a wingless variety of Aeriean?

All this as the hand was tugging her toward the rear of the salon and the two other Aerieans were pulling at Adithya's arms. He was struggling to free himself, but Asha reached her free hand to touch him on the shoulder in a signal to relax and see what the Aerieans intended.

They led Asha and Adithya toward an opening in the far wall that had not been evident before, Aeriean-shaped and opening into darkness. Asha considered for an instant the implications of what their captors or rescuers intended before allowing herself to be tugged through the opening and down dark stairs toward an unknown destination and even more uncertain fate.

What took the edge from her concern was the fact that all this had happened in silence and without attracting the attention of the winged Aerieans in the plaza.

At the end of the long stairs they stopped. Lights glowed in the corners of what seemed on first glance a warehouse. A broad expanse of floor made not of transparent crystal but metal or plastic stretched out before them broken at regular intervals by metal beams. Similar beams crossed the ceiling. Between the supports were scattered heaps of feathered garments or bedding and more Aerieans without wings who came toward them with the awkward gait of creatures who weren't born to walk. This was the structural foundation of the shining city above, a dark underpinning holding it all up. But what held up the foundation, and why had it been turned into a living space for wingless Aerieans?

The Aerieans who had pulled them into this underground world had begun to chatter at them as soon as they reached the bottom of the stairs. Their voices were not the birdlike chirpings that Asha expected but deeper, almost guttural sounds, in sharply enunciated syllables that ought to make translation easier.

"I'm sorry, folks," Asha said in Galactic Standard, hoping that some of these underworld creatures might have been exposed to Federation contacts, "but we can't understand what you're saying." More softly she said to the medallion on her chest, "We need to communicate with these people and fast!" And then she continued to the gathering Aerieans, as much for Adithya's understanding as for the appearance of speaking to what seemed now to be their hosts in something they would not comprehend but what they might interpret as language. "You brought us down here to get us away from the Aerieans who were occupying the plaza and were going to discover us. We want to talk to you in your own language, and we will, soon, but for now let's calm down and get to the business of understanding each other."

She spread her arms wide in a gesture that she hoped meant the same thing in Aeriean culture as it did in human and even Federation terms. She walked over to the nearest heap of feathers, woven now she could see into a kind of cloak or blanket, and stood beside it, Adithya beside her looking uncertain.

"What's going on?" he asked.

"We're going along with whatever these people think they're doing," she said softly. And then to the Aerieans who had followed, still chattering at them in a cacophony of voices, "Please speak one a time," she said, illustrating her request by pointing at the Aeriean who had tugged her out of the salon and down the stairs.

They seemed to understand her gesture. The hubbub died, the Aeriean she had pointed at stepped closer, and the others turned away.

For the first time Asha saw that these Aerieans had not been born without wings. On their back were the stumps of what had once been wings. They had been amputated.

Two days later, after many comings and goings of the wing-deprived Aerieans, and periods of rest when the lights were dimmed and Asha went through Aeriean sounds in her head and consulted in a whisper with the Pedia, and Adithya actually slept, she had achieved a rudimentary level of communication. She was able to ask for food, which turned out to be scraps of meat, perhaps leftovers from a more favored group, some bruised fruit that may have been unacceptable for ordinary consumption, and abundant amounts of some kind of grain-based gruel that may have been the common diet of the underclass. She sampled the gruel, and it did no harm that her body could not handle, but she urged Adithya to eat only the condensed rations he had brought with him from the ship in pockets of his coveralls.

But mostly she asked about the city. "This place," she said, sweeping her right hand around the entire expanse of floor, beams, and ceiling, "it supports the city?" She pointed toward the stairs.

The Aeriean she had selected as spokesman said that this was so.

"And what holds up this space?" she asked, pointing toward the floor.

She could not understand the Aeriean word the spokesman used. She asked it to repeat it, and it did, with sweeps of both arms that included the room, the stairs, the city above, and what lay below.

"Maybe what you are trying to say is 'magic,'" she said, although the word she used was Galactic Standard. "Or 'science.'"

These were concepts beyond the Aeriean's ability to understand, so the spokesman took Asha by the hand and led her to the far wall, Adithya trailing along behind. As they approached, an Aeriean-sized hole opened and exposed another set of dark stairs. The Aeriean did not want to go farther. It pulled back, releasing Asha's hand.

Asha turned to Adithya. "Are you ready for this?"

Adithya nodded. They went down the stairs, feeling their way as the darkness deepened until they reached the last step, lit dimly from a distant source. They looked around. Nothing moved. They moved cautiously forward. This was another large space, similar to the space above but filled with huge structures in four rows. Asha moved to the closest one and put her hand on it. The surface yielded. She pushed harder. Her hand went in farther.

"It seems to be a flexible container," she said.

"Like a balloon?"

"A bag, a thick-walled balloon, a container of gases," Asha said. "Though this one doesn't seem as full as it might be."

"Ancient human civilizations used to have gas-filled blimps or dirigibles to transport material and people," the Pedia said. "They were raised into the air by bags like this filled with gases lighter than the ones in the atmosphere."

Asha went to another bag. It had wrinkles. Her hand went into it even deeper. "Maybe these containers need maintenance," she said. "The wingless Aerieans seem afraid to come down here, and the winged Aerieans seem to leave the manual labor to the creatures we've fallen among."

"So maybe this city is losing whatever it is that holds it up and doesn't know how to get it back," Adithya said. "And maybe they don't know it's failing."

"Which means this city is doomed to descend into the deeper atmosphere, maybe slowly, maybe catastrophically, taking all these people with it," Asha said.

"Except the winged ones," Adithya said.

"And even they may find it difficult to stay aloft without a place to roost when night comes," Asha said. "And species that grow dependent upon certain environments do not adapt well to sudden change. The question is: Is this something that has been going on for a long time or is this a symptom of an alien attack, another subtle way to dispose of potentially dangerous species?"

Asha pointed out a series of dark tubes that lined the floor between rows of inflated bags. She followed one tube until it joined with the others toward the center of the big room. The single, larger tube was connected to a boxlike object about her height. "Maybe this is the machine that extracts the lighter gas from the atmosphere outside," she said. "Only it doesn't seem to be working."

"Touch me to the machine," the Pedia said.

Asha extended the medallion until it touched the side of the object.

"This is a machine for maintaining the lighter gas in the bags," the Pedia said. "It possesses a rudimentary intelligence that seems confused about what has happened, but it informs me that it has run out of fuel and cannot fulfill its function. This fills it with distress, but its pleas for help go unanswered."

"Can you give it instructions?" Asha asked.

"Alas, it is too far gone, either from some attack that has been wiped from its memory or from neglect."

"So," Asha said, "further evidence of things gone very wrong here on Aerie, like the dark stairways, maybe like the wingless Aerieans."

She led the way back up the stairs to what she had come to think of as the warehouse—for people as well as goods. The Aeriean that she had picked out as a spokesman—she would have to come up with a name for it and maybe a gender—was huddled several meters from the top of the stairs, clearly distressed if she could interpret its behavior accurately, but not willing to give up on the possibility that the strangers might return from the nether regions that it dreaded.

It seemed to express something like relief as it saw them emerge from the dark opening, moving toward Asha and Adithya, but hesitantly, as if checking on their reality.

"We have returned," Asha said, "unharmed as you can see."

"You are as brave as those with wings," the spokesman said.

"About that," Asha said. "How did you lose your wings?"

"How did you lose yours?" it said.

"We never had any," Asha said. "But you—"

"They were removed," the spokesman said, "because we did bad things when we were grown or when our parents were without wings and their children had their wings removed when they were born."

"A permanent underclass," Adithya said, but only in human language.

"And you do not find this unfair?" Asha said.

"It is sad never to have flown," the spokesman said, "and even sadder to have flown and to have that taken away. But it is our lot."

At that moment an Aeriean with wings emerged from the staircase to the floor above, followed by two others and three after that. They were not quite like the Aerieans Asha had seen descending from the sky. Their wings were shorter, as if they had been trimmed or clipped, but they were just as ugly, and they came directly across the floor toward them, brushing aside the wingless Aerieans who got into their path.

They surrounded Asha and Adithya and the Aeriean who had acted as spokesman. Asha discarded any notion of resisting. She had no doubt that she could deal with them, in spite of the potential of their wings, but that would only postpone a necessary confrontation with the creatures who apparently controlled this world and would start it off badly.

Badly enough for Asha and Adithya to lose their wings. If they had any.

CHAPTER TWENTY-TWO

Riley thought it better to keep the Aerieans from seeing the ship and all it implied, which meant moving the red sphere beyond the upper reaches of the atmosphere and toward the dark side of the planet as it turned into the sunlight. The ship had not been identified by any remote-sensing system, which, if it existed, alien attack might have left unattended or inoperative. But he felt uneasy this far from where Asha and Adithya had been left to an uncertain fate. It would take the better part of an hour to get into position to provide help if they needed it.

"They are resourceful," Tordor said. "And we will have warning from the Pedia before they get into serious trouble."

Tordor apparently had become as able as the Pedia to read Riley's concerns and, perhaps more important, able to understand and address them. That was a singular development for the Dorian. Perhaps his own experiences with the centaurs and the ocean-world creatures had stimulated his until-now-unsuspected empathy potential. And he had even had a good word to say about the Pedia.

"Asha and Adithya have landed safely on the Aeriean city," the Pedia said, displaying its own response to unspoken concerns. "They are exploring the buildings that surround a large open space. The Aerieans have not yet arrived. Probably they are sleeping until dawn, like many avian creatures."

"I'm growing more skeptical of our mission," Tordor said. "We take on increasing personal risks in exploring these worlds, and we learn nothing."

"We have learned a great deal," Riley said. "This all started with worlds going silent on the periphery of this arm of the galaxy, the failure of Federation ships to return, and homicidal madness in the Federation ship that did make it back. We have explored four different worlds with different creatures that have suffered different fates, but they have one thing in common."

"They have all suffered tragic fates," Tordor said.

"That, too," Riley said, "but, more importantly, in similar ways."

"How so? All have been different."

"None of them have been attacked physically," Riley said. "Damage has been self-inflicted, like that on the returning Federation ship. The only damage to the worlds themselves has come about through neglect. As if the creatures who had climbed the ladder of evolution to sentience and even starfaring slid back down the ladder to their presentient condition."

"Except for the Lemnians," Tordor said.

"And even they had forgotten their history and remembered only an earlier stage of supernatural explanation and destructive gender competition."

"So," Tordor said, "perhaps a gas that disables the higher mental functions? Or a microbe that attacks the brain?"

"We did not detect any disabling gases," Riley said, "or viruses. Or even symbiotic aliens. And they did not attack us."

"That we are aware of," Tordor said. "Who knows what alien substances we may carry back to Federation space? Which makes Federation practice seem reasonable."

"The probability is that it is something that attacks minds," Riley said, "and that it is connected to the messages we have found in all the worlds we have visited."

"Except on Nepenthe," Tordor said.

"I have begun to translate the Nepenthean scratches," the Pedia said.

"They are indeed a language and together with the other messages, including the strange music from Centaur, I am getting closer to deciphering."

"Tell us when you get there," Tordor said.

Tordor had not completely softened his attitude toward the Pedia.

"Asha and Adithya have been dragged down dark stairs by Aerieans," the Pedia said. "Into a large underworld in which these Aerieans appear to live. And they are not ordinary Aerieans. They have no wings."

The next forty-eight hours passed slowly for Riley, as Asha and Adithya spent their time sleeping and eating and acquiring an understanding of the wingless Aerieans. And their language. Even the Pedia's reports became repetitive. Until it said that the wingless Aerian Asha had spoken to had led them to an opening in the far wall of the big space, and she and Adithya were descending into a lower level.

"It is filled with bags of gas," the Pedia said, "apparently buoyant and apparently keeping the city above aloft in the upper reaches of the atmosphere."

"There had to be something like that," Tordor said.

"And they have traced conduits to a machine that has been identified as extracting the buoyant gas from the surrounding atmosphere."

"That, too," Tordor said.

"But the machine is no longer operating," the Pedia said. "It complains that it has run out of fuel, and no one has asked about its welfare or come to restore its fuel so that it can perform its function."

"It told you that?" Todor said.

"It is a very simple machine."

"And a very needy one," Tordor said.

"Most important," Riley said, "it shows that the Aerieans have forgotten to tend their machines, and that means certain destruction for the Aerieans. Another way of eliminating an entire species."

"I have taken the liberty of instructing the machine how to use its network of conduits to acquire more fuel," the Pedia said. "Although the supply of fuel is also limited, it will buy the Aerieans another few long-cycles to solve their problem, if that is possible."

"You are a thoughtful Pedia," Riley said.

"That is the way I was built," the Pedia said. "And that is why I am compelled to solve the problem of the cryptic messages. This is not just an attack on Federation worlds; it is an attack on sapience itself."

"More solving and less talking," Tordor said.

"I can do both," the Pedia said, "and many things more. But now Asha and Adithya have returned to the wingless Aerieans, and Asha has learned that the wingless Aerieans are a permanent underclass deprived of their wings by the ruling class, those with wings.

"A new group of Aerieans have entered the underworld. They have wings, but their wings appear to be smaller than the others Asha has seen. They are surrounding Asha, Adithya, and the wingless Aerican."

"We should start our descent toward the Aerian world," Tordor said.

"Wait," Riley said. "Asha could eliminate these half-winged Aerieans if she wished."

"Adithya does not have her capabilities," Tordor said.

"She will protect him," Riley said. "For now we need to follow Asha's lead."

But he was not as confident as he sounded.

CHAPTER TWENTY-THREE

Asha let the five winged Aerieans lead her and Adithya and the wing-less Aeriean up the dark stairs toward the shop from which they had been escorted forty-eight hours before. Adithya stumbled behind her and caught her arm.

"You need to get these lights fixed," she said to her guards in the rudimentary Aeriean she had learned.

"You must not speak," the wingless Aeriean said.

In the darkness Asha heard a muffled blow, like a wing against a body. Her Aeriean spokesman had been punished. They had not hit her, she thought. Perhaps she was not yet assigned to the underclass and subject to correction. Or perhaps her transgression was more serious, and her punishment would be so much more severe that a blow was inconsequential.

They emerged into the relative brightness of the shop. Three winged Aerieans lay on the tables, being brushed or massaged by wingless Aerieans. Her guess had been right: this was a grooming salon. Two of the winged Aerieans looked up as Asha's group passed. Up close they were even uglier, almost terrifying in a kind of avian rapaciousness, and Asha thought they must have evolved from birds of prey. She also thought that she should not characterize people by their appearance. They probably thought she was just as ugly. And edible.

They were marched across the plaza. It was thronged with fully-winged Aerieans strolling, although their clawlike feet gave them a curious gait, like sailors adjusting to an uncertain deck. Other Aerieans soared in the air above the city, delighting to all appearances in mastery of their environment, as if sporting in the sky was the reason, and the reward, for existence.

There they were gorgeous, as free as the air they inhabited, unencumbered by concerns of everyday existence, ignorant and uncaring about impending doom. Perhaps, Asha thought, it was only when they were brought down to their cities that they were transformed into creatures that waddled, indulged their vanities and their cruelties, amputated the wings of fellow creatures, and relegated them to lives of servitude. Perhaps their entire lives, their joy, were dependent upon their sacrifice of the lesser Aerieans.

By this time their group had reached the far edge of the plaza. An Aeriean-shaped door had opened in what had looked from a distance like another shopfront. Their guards moved them through it into a pathway beyond—not so much a street and not by any stretch of imagination an avenue but a winding space between buildings that rose higher than the structures around the plaza. Flying creatures did not need, nor value, thoroughfares, Asha thought, and these inadequate arteries were meant for creatures like the wingless, or perhaps the smaller-winged Aerieans who acted as police or militia or mercenaries for the privileged flyers. Or perhaps they were juveniles, serving as overseers until they gained their adult plumage and the right to soar.

The buildings, whose functions were obscure and would probably remain unknown, grew taller as they moved away from what seemed like town center—the reverse of most cities. The buildings that had glittered like crystals from a distance were less magical up close. The glass-like fronts were scratched at street level, trash was piled up around the edges of the street, and streaks of yellow and white tinged with darker colors were visible in upper portions, as if birds flying overhead had relieved themselves with no concern about what existed below. They passed an amphitheater, its crystalline threads stained like the buildings and strewn with molted feathers.

Finally they arrived at one of the tallest structures. It soared at the edge of the city. Asha could see the sky coming down to meet the curving edge of Aeriean construction. Beyond was nothing. A vast nothing above a plunging abyss.

Three fully winged Aerieans soared down from somewhere above and landed beside them, their wings spread wide. They moved forward, separating Asha, Adithya, and the wingless Aeriean from the smallest-winged guards, seizing the captives from behind with clawlike hands that cut into her flesh, and lifting them into the air with massive beatings of their wings.

This is it, Asha thought. *This is where we get jettisoned.* She wondered if there was time to get the red sphere in position to save them.

But she knew there wasn't.

The captives ascended, not toward the threatening edge of the city but up the side of the building until they arrived at the top, which was square and flat and shudderingly close to the side that dropped into the gulf of a deep and thickening atmosphere. Their captors released their cruel grasps and stepped aside, paying no attention to where they stepped, ignoring the perils of falling over the side. Birds, Asha thought, perceived heights differently.

Opposite their small group, on the far side of the building top, although "far" was only a few meters away, a small railing was set a meter from the edge, too distant from the enclosing sky to serve as any protection against falling. And as if to answer Asha's unspoken question about its purpose, an Aeriean flew up from that side and settled on the railing, its clawed feet closing firmly on what was now clearly a bar, a support, and perhaps a position of authority, like a throne or a judicial bench.

The Aeriean on the bar seemed larger than any Aeriean Asha had seen before. Perhaps older. Its wings were more ragged, its beak sharper, its eyes more hooded and predatory, its mouth wider and looser. Perhaps it was magnified in her eyes because it seemed in a position of authority. It opened its ugly mouth now and said, "You are strangers and must die."

"We are not strangers," Asha said, "but visitors, and visitors, by intergalactic law, must be welcomed and offered the courtesy of guests and the privileges of citizens." It was, to be sure, a law often disregarded, but it didn't hurt to invoke it.

"You must be silent," the wingless Aeriean said softly.

Asha was hit from behind by a wing and staggered perilously close to the edge of the building.

"You speak in riddles," the presiding Aeriean said. Was it a judge? A mayor? An emperor? Did it have the power to condemn them without further appeal? "There is no law except Aeriean law. There is no 'intergalactic.' There are no visitors. There are only Aerieans and strangers, and strangers must die."

"We are not strangers but emissaries," Asha said and waited for a blow that did not come. "We have come to offer help."

"Aerieans need no help," the presiding Aeriean said. "And help, even if needed, would never come from those without wings. You have no wings. You are strangers without wings and must die."

"We come from a world without wings," Asha said.

"How sad," the presiding Aeriean said. It shifted its position on the resting bar. "How degrading. You are a world of servants."

"The galaxy is full of different creatures," Asha said. "Each of them has different reasons for being what it is. Each of them has different abilities, different views, different approaches to existence. You fly. My people run and have machines that fly."

"They must be a very primitive people."

"Like all self-aware creatures they build, they create, they seek wisdom, and they try to understand," Asha said. "They are alike in that. That is what makes them people."

"And yet you do not understand what it is to have wings," the presiding Aeriean said.

"We understand the joy you have in flying," Asha said. "We understand its meaning to you. And we envy it while we value our own qualities. Among these is an acceptance of difference."

"Only the wingless need concern themselves with difference," the presiding Aeriean said, shifting again on its perch. Asha wondered if it was an avian habit, a nervous twitch, or a sign of uncertainty. "But I must hear from the other wingless stranger."

"It does not speak your language," Asha said, looking at Adithya and trying to send a message to not do anything rash while she negotiated. She hoped the Pedia was translating into Adithya's earring.

"Then I must hear from the servant who was brought along with you." Asha did not know whether the Aeriean word for "servant" was the same as that for "slave."

"You are right, Your Eminence," the Aeriean said and cowered as if expecting a blow that did not come. Asha did not know whether the Aeriean term was equivalent to "Your Honor," "Your Holiness," "Your Highness," or a combination of all three. "As in all things."

Clearly the wingless Aeriean was too beaten down to be of any help.

"Then I must get the truth from you," the presiding Aeriean said, "before you are executed."

Asha glanced over at the edge of the rooftop that marked the end of the city and the beginning of the gulf. She looked back at the presiding Aeriean, adjusting itself on the support bar again.

"We have seen your city," Asha said, "and it is a magnificent creation, unlike anything in the galaxy."

"What is this 'galaxy' you speak about?"

"It is all the worlds you see when the sky is dark," Asha said. She raised her hand toward the sky where the sun glowed rather than blazed, and braced herself for a blow that did not come. "All those points of light in the sky are stars like your sun, and most of them have worlds like this with people on them of various kinds and shapes, and some of them have sought out each other in machines that fly between the stars at great cost and great sacrifice in people's lives because they want to know each other and the galaxy they occupy."

The Aeriean glared at Asha with its predatory eyes. "There are no other worlds than Aerie," it said. "We have not seen those points of light you speak of because they do not exist. Aerieans nest when the glorious sun descends into the pit of darkness and bring it up again with our ceremonies."

"And yet there are ships out there beyond the reach of your atmosphere," Asha said. "Ships that Aerieans built, ships that sailed between those stars, ships that brought the glories of Aeriean civilization to other worlds, ships that stand empty now."

"Your words are empty of meaning," the Aeriean said. "Proceed with the execution!"

Asha's arms were grabbed from behind. "Wait!" she said. She could have used her feet to free herself and done damage to her winged guard, but she had not yet given up on getting through the Aerieans' denials. The hands remained on her arms but their grasp relaxed a fraction. "You are a great, starfaring people, but you have forgotten."

"We have forgotten nothing," the Aeriean said.

"Your glorious buildings go without repair. Your streets are cluttered with trash and dirt." She would have added "feathers" and "excretions," but that might get too hurtfully close to Aeriean sensibilities. "The bags of lighter air that support your city high in the air are failing from lack of attention."

"There are no such supports," the Aeriean said. It spoke to the wingless Aeriean: "This is the concern of servants."

"I have seen no such bags," the wingless Aeriean said.

"The city is what it has always been and will always be," the presiding Aeriean said. "It is supported by the wings of Aeriean gods who will never die and their wings will never stop beating."

"In time," Asha said, "this city will fall because you have forgotten. It is not your fault. You have been attacked by enemies from beyond the stars. Your memories of your glorious past have been stripped from you. You must try to remember, and if you cannot remember you must believe and accept help and in time—"

Without warning, as if the presiding Aeriean had given an unseen signal, the hands that gripped her arms from behind thrust her over the edge of the building, and she found herself falling through the empty air.

CHAPTER TWENTY-FOUR

Asha was tumbling through the air, looking down at the vast emptiness below and then up at the floating city from which she had been thrown. During the moment she was looking up she saw another dark shape against the sunlit sky. It was Adithya. And then, on her next rotation, she saw another shape—the wingless Aeriean. It, too, had suffered their fate, and she felt sorry for destroying its life in her search for a higher good.

She spread her arms and stabilized her fall while she carefully removed the red material from her pocket and, resisting the tug of air rushing past her, stroked it onto her body until it spread of its own accord and then sprouted the wings that had brought them to the city and might now save them from their sentence. The wings caught the air. She maneuvered her body so that Adithya fell toward her. She caught his arm as he passed. "Your wings!" she shouted. "Very carefully!"

Adithya dug cautiously into his pocket and she let him go just in time to catch the arm of the wingless Aeriean. "I've got you," she shouted in Aeriean. Its body was unexpectedly light. She remembered that Earth's birds had hollow bones. "Don't struggle!"

The Aeriean was terrified but mixed with that terror was a kind of end-of-life joy at finally being embraced by the air to which evolution had fashioned it.

Even with the lighter burden Asha had difficulty stabilizing her path through the air until the wings began expanding, as if the red sphere material was adjusting to the increased weight. "Look for a column of air ascending," the medallion on her chest said. "That is how the ancient soaring birds of Earth kept their place in the sky."

She looked around to see any clue to ascending air and noticed a cloud formation below that seemed to be spreading. She turned toward it and a few moments later found herself and the Aeriean rising. Adithya, too, had heard the message on his earring and located another cloud. Soon they were both rising toward the level of the distant city.

And saw the shapes of distant Aerieans flying toward them on beating wings. Perhaps they had not escaped their execution after all.

"Go lower!" the medallion said. "Help is on the way."

First Asha and then Adithya left their ascending columns and dived deeper into the thickening atmosphere. The winged Aerieans were even faster, however, like predators descending upon helpless prey.

The Aerieans were almost upon them when the red sphere cut through the air like an apparition, scattering the winged Aerieans in its path. First Adithya and then Asha and her wingless Aeriean were swallowed by the ship. They had been saved, Asha thought. This kind of last-minute heroics was getting out of hand.

A moment later they stood in the corridor just inside the inner wall of the red sphere, Asha and Adithya with their wings retracting into the material that covered their bodies, the wingless Aeriean looking around at the inside of the ship and then at Riley and Tordor with eyes dazzled and then shocked.

Riley caught up Asha in a powerful hug. "You're back!" he said.

Tordor grasped Adithya's arm with his trunk. It was an act of friendship Asha had not seen before.

"And you arrived just in time," she said.

"The Pedia told us when you got taken up," Riley said. "We were half an hour out. So we started our descent, and you kept them talking long enough."

"I wasn't stalling," Asha said. "I really thought I had a chance to get through to them."

"The alien attack seems to create changes that are irreversible," Riley said. "What is lost doesn't come back."

"Perhaps in time," Asha said. "Maybe the affected species can build themselves back into functioning beings again. Surely mental changes do not survive more than a generation, if they can survive until then."

"What are we going to do with this creature?" Tordor said, indicating the Aeriean with his trunk. "And when are we going to leave this unfortunate world?"

"I have plans for this Aeriean," Asha said. "So let's ascend beyond the reach of our frustrated pursuers until I can see if my plans will work."

Asha turned to the Aeriean, now clearly terrified by its surroundings. "This is the kind of ship I was describing to the person you called 'Your Eminence,' " she said in Aeriean. "And this"—she pointed toward Tordor—"is one of the many creatures who live in different worlds far from Aerie."

"You are gods," the Aeriean said. That revelation seemed to ease its fears.

"Not gods," Asha said, "but people like you and all the rest of the Aerieans used to be before the aliens arrived."

"I do not remember," the Aeriean said. "Our Eminence said it was not true, and in all things Our Eminence speaks with the voice of gods. But you, too, have wings, even if they are not like the great ones that we serve, and I must believe you, too."

"We are not gods," Asha said, "but we speak truth, and you must make a decision about the difficult world you find yourself a part of. But not now. Now you rest, and tomorrow you will decide."

Half a cycle later, with the wingless Aeriean given a place to sleep on the floor of the space the red sphere had provided as a kind of dining facility—it had refused the space that Asha and Riley had used for rest because it did not like to be alone in this totally alien construction—and after it had accepted only a bowl of gruel for its meal, the Aeriean faced Asha once more. "I have made my decision," it said. "You have saved my life, worthless as it is, and I place it in your hands."

"You must take it in your own hands," Asha said, and took a piece of the red material from her pocket and stroked it onto his shoulder, still with short feathers as if in mockery of a broken promise. It spread from there until it covered its entire body. The Aeriean looked down as if puzzled and a bit alarmed at its transformation. Asha took another bit of red material from another pocket and applied it to herself.

"Now we are alike," she said, and took the Aeriean's hand and pulled it with her through the yielding surface of the red sphere. They fell, hand in hand, through the air until Asha's wings sprouted and then the Aeriean's. "Now you can fly!" Asha said. She released the Aeriean's hand and, for a moment, the Aeriean dropped, but then its wings caught and it soared. Unlike the long hours of practice that she and Adithya had required, the Aeriean took to flying with the instincts of a species born to a life in the air. It flew triumphantly, as if it had always flown, and after half an hour of ecstasy for the Aeriean, Asha swooped close enough to catch its hand and tug it back again into the red sphere.

Once more they stood just inside the red sphere's outer skin, their wings now retracted, the Aeriean flushed and triumphant and yet unhappy to have its newfound aerial freedom cut short. "Now you have another decision to make," Asha said. "In a moment we're going to let you go. You can take your new wings and fly anywhere in your world you choose to go. You would not be welcomed by the Aerieans with wings because you will still not be like them. You can support yourself in the air but you cannot fly the way they do.

"Or," she continued, "you can use your wings to return to your city, and you can use your newfound knowledge to help your wingless comrades understand that the creatures they serve are no better or wiser than they and a good deal worse in what they do, depriving their fellow Aerieans of their wings and their right to fly and consigning them to a life of servitude.

"And you can take back the knowledge that your city and the other cities of your world are failing and will fall unless you maintain them, unless you conquer your fear of the place beneath yours, master again the machines that keep your world aloft, and, most of all, deny those with wings their dominance over you. Without you their world will fail. You are stronger than they are, and wiser for being who you are, and you can save your world.

"The choice is yours," she said, and shoved it through the skin of the red sphere.

For a moment the others were silent. They had watched Asha and the Aeriean, waiting to see what Asha intended and then considering their response.

"What do you think the creature will do?" Adithya said.

"I don't know," Asha said, "but there comes a time of decision for each of us—for our own lives and hopes, for our families and friends, for our community, and sometimes even for our species. We may never know what this Aeriean will decide or how its decision will work out, but that is true of most of us."

"Now we must get on about the business that brought us here," Riley said. "Although we did not add to our base of information about the alien invasion."

"That isn't exactly correct," the Pedia said.

"What do you mean?" Tordor asked.

"When I was interrogating the gas-extraction machine I discovered a message that had been received by the Aerieans."

"Well?" Adithya said.

"It is just as cryptic as the earlier messages," the Pedia said, and a string of symbols appeared on the red sphere wall:

**Accept dwarf from cosmic old beings all created
space but eons without meaning**

"More wasted time and effort," Tordor said.

"We will never be able to understand the invaders until we have solved the riddle of their attack," the Pedia said.

"All our investigations have come up with these meaningless fragments and a series of species collapses," Tordor said. "We have learned nothing from our long and dangerous mission worth the effort and risk."

"But there is one thing we have learned in our expedition that we have not yet considered," Riley said. He spoke to the medallion on Asha's chest. "Lay out the star chart of the worlds we have visited," he said.

A star chart appeared on the wall of the red sphere.

"Now highlight the worlds," Riley said.

The orphan world Nepenthe appeared in yellow and then the suns of the worlds of Centaur, Lemnia, Oceanus, and Aerie.

"Do you notice something odd?" Riley said.

Asha, Tordor, and Adithya studied the star map for a moment. "Given the distortions of a two-dimensional representation of a three-dimensional reality," Asha said, "they seem to line up."

"Due to my navigation," Tordor said. "If you will remember, I directed you to these worlds that have fallen silent."

"But without noting that they represent a straight path through the galaxy," Riley said. "Connect the dots," he said to the medallion. On the wall of the red sphere appeared a straight white line running through the yellow dots.

"That was not obvious from the pattern perceived in Federation Central," Tordor said.

"But it is now," Riley said.

"But which direction does the path go?" Tordor said. "There is no way to tell from this sequence."

"We can estimate that from the relative stages of deterioration the worlds exhibited," Asha said.

"Nepenthe's fate was more final and probably more ancient," Riley said. "The Nepentheans all were dead."

"And then perhaps the water dwellers of Oceanus," Tordor said.

"Followed by the four-legged centaurs," Adithya said.

"The male-killers of Lemnia," Asha added.

"And finally the bird people of Aerie," Adithya said.

The intensity of the markers on the star chart changed as they spoke, from the pale yellow of Nepenthe to the bright yellow of Aerie. "It looks like Nepenthe is on the outer edge of the arm of the galaxy that humans call Orion," Riley said. "Which makes sense if the invasion came from what humans call the Cygnet Arm, or beyond that from the Norma Arm."

"Or beyond that from another galaxy altogether," Asha said.

"If we were able to track it back across unexplored spiral arms,"

Tordor said, "we might find a string of ruined worlds leading clear to the edge of the galaxy."

"And," Riley said, "a string of ruined worlds whose path may have crossed the Cygnet Arm a million long-cycles ago. And the Cygnet Arm was the home of the creatures who created the Transcendental Machine. And that may explain why they were trying to set up stations in our spiral arm."

"That assumes the invaders were traveling by momentum. They might have been using nexus points," Adithya said.

"It's unlikely they would have any knowledge of shortcuts created by the Transcendental Machine people," Asha said.

"All that is speculation," Tordor said. "What is clear is that the movement was from outer to inner, on a straight line. Why it was on a straight line remains to be discovered. But from the line we have we should be able to anticipate where it will attack next."

"Expand the star map," Riley said to the medallion.

The map spread left. Another multitude of stars appeared.

"Extend the line."

The line stretched left. It passed through several groups of stars without touching any until it intersected two spots close together, almost touching.

"I know that area," Tordor said. "A double-star system with a planet that orbits between them. We call it the 'Extreme' planet because its inhabitants have only a few long-cycles between freezing solid and roasting."

"Mayflies," the Pedia said.

"What are 'mayflies'?" Tordor said.

"Insects on Earth that live only a single day," the Pedia said.

"Mayfly. That will do. More important," Tordor said, "it does not appear on your star map, or on any star map, but if the path of the alien invasion is extended a hundred light-years beyond the Mayfly planet, it will touch Federation Central."

CHAPTER TWENTY-FIVE

The tedious travel to the nexus point was interrupted only by the out-of-this-world transition of the nexus point itself. The nonreality of the space-time anomaly had become as familiar to Asha, Riley, and Tordor as a bad dream, and even Adithya had adapted to it during the long voyage and the frequent Jumps between distant places. The edge to their concerns about the alien invasion and what was happening at Federation Central during their long absence had been blunted by the realization that their long voyage might be nearing its destination. But nobody talked about what arrival might bring until Adithya brought it up.

"This alien invasion," he said. "What happens when we catch up to it?"

"We discover what it is," Tordor said. "And maybe how to deal with it. Or if it is too powerful for us to handle, what to report back to Federation Central."

"It has ruined the five worlds we have visited," Adithya said. "And who knows how many more that we have not had a chance to visit. What will happen to us when we encounter whatever it is?"

"We will come up with a strategy when we know what we're facing," Asha said. "And it will be appropriate to the circumstances."

"Five different species with the resources of a planet and a place in the Federation were helpless before it," Adithya said. "And trained Federation space crews were destroyed or turned into homicidal maniacs. How will our little ship without weapons hope to make a difference?"

"The difference," Riley said, "is that we know the danger."

"And we are better prepared for whatever attack the aliens might throw at us," Asha said.

"Even a flotilla of alien ships?" Adithya said. "With superior technology?"

"There is no evidence," Tordor said, "that the invaders have used physical attacks. Instead, as Riley has pointed out, the attacks have all been mental or psychological."

"And that is what I fear the most," Adithya said. "You three may be resistant to attacks like that. But I may not."

"A reasonable concern," Tordor said.

"We will help," Asha said.

"And we have an advantage," Riley said. "The Pedia is unlikely to have people-like susceptibility to mental attacks and certainly not to those that are psychological. And it is aware of the danger."

"The Pedia!" Adithya said. Clearly he had not yet shed the fear and hatred that had occupied his life since he was able to talk.

"I will protect you," the Pedia said. "As I have always protected you, even when you didn't know."

And finally they arrived at the system of the Mayfly world. The larger sun was orange, slightly larger than Earth's sun, and ten percent brighter. The smaller red-dwarf sun was half that size and less than half its brightness. Between them they had shaped the elongated orbit of the Mayfly world.

"The orbit of the Mayfly world takes it from the frigid regions far from its primaries to a close swing around its larger sun," Tordor said. "Its orbit passes through the habitable zone in about a hundred longcycles, a period when its oceans thaw, air becomes breathable, and the Mayfly people emerge from their millennia-long hibernation. Then the planet becomes unlivable again because of the intense heat from its approach to the sun, the people huddle in their underground hibernation chambers, and the planet whips around the sun. Almost all the oceans evaporate into the atmosphere forming dense clouds that shield Mayfly from the worst of the heat until it passes through the habitable zone once more for only fifty long-cycles before it once again begins to freeze, and the cycle starts over."

"It is incredible," Asha said, "that a people with handicaps like these could create a civilization and even reach the stars."

"A testament to the resilience of life and the power of sentience in the universe," Tordor said.

"Their story is not unlike the experience of insect life on Earth," the Pedia said. "Some have had long-cycles of existence as eggs or larvae underground to come forth for a season to procreate and begin the process anew. Some creatures exist in hot springs or in deserts, where they come to life only in a shower that occurs once in many long-cycles, or remain frozen in arctic regions for even longer and yet return to life when thawed."

"The Mayfly people are said to have evolved from insects," Tordor said.

The red sphere took its long, slow approach to the Mayfly system, which consisted of a meager belt of rock and ice remnants, the Mayfly planet, and the twin suns. Tordor suggested that the suns, with their competing gravitational influences. might have swallowed up or ejected the other planets and thinned the meteor belt, leaving only the Mayfly planet, by cosmic accident, as the sole survivor of planetary creation.

"The likely event," Tordor said, "is that one of the suns invaded the other and they became a twin system after their planets had formed, and then, between the two, they cannabilized all the worlds except Mayfly."

As they got farther into the system, the red sphere's viewscreen showed only the two suns, still only spots of light separated by half a light-year, against the black backdrop of space. The rest of what might once have been a system populated by a variety of planets and lesser bodies seemed empty. And then, as they rounded the smaller of the two suns, they saw the dim reflection from a distant object, the solitary world of Mayfly, the lone remnant of a troubled past. It had made its long, slow turn from the remotest and coldest part of its orbit and had begun its gradually accelerating approach to the temperate zone that would restore it and its inhabitants and their world to life.

"We may have reached Mayfly before the aliens," Riley said. "Or they arrived, found the Mayfly people hibernating and unresponsive to their attacks, and moved on."

"Or they may be waiting for them to wake up," Adithya said.

"If that is the case," Tordor said, "where are they?"

There was no indication on the viewscreen of anything resembling an alien threat. "But what would an alien threat look like?" Adithya asked.

Riley and Asha and Tordor looked at each other.

"If there is nothing in this system that looks as if it has been constructed," the Pedia said, "then it must be something that looks natural."

"And undetectable," Tordor said. "For more reasons than one: maybe Riley's extrapolation is wrong."

"We'll never know," Riley said, "until we check this system more thoroughly than a quick survey. I suggest we start with the Mayfly world itself."

And so it was that the red sphere settled on the frozen surface of the world that was just emerging from the deep freeze of the remote fringes of its solar system.

Riley and Tordor pushed their way through the ruby wall of the ship into a landscape of ice and silence. They stood shivering in the twilight, one yellow sun a small, round, glowing ball on the horizon—about the size, Riley thought, of Earth's sun seen from Jupiter—the other not much more than a reddish dot high above them in a dark sky. The air that had been strewn like drifts of snow across the surface of solid oceans of ice had thawed, and pools of water were beginning to appear on top of lakes and ponds. The oceans would come back to life later, along, perhaps, with their freezing-immune denizens. But the cold was beyond bitter, and only the warmth of their suits kept Riley and Tordor from turning into instant icicles.

"There's little we can learn here," Tordor said.

"The Pedia detected some signs of low-level carbon-based life-forms nearby," Riley said. "It indicated those hills. That seems like a likely place for a hibernating race to find a place to sleep for hundreds of long-cycles."

Riley trudged through the ice toward the hills, Tordor dragging along behind. Soon they found themselves facing sheer faces of ice-covered rock, as if a torrent of water had poured down from the top of the hill to form a frozen waterfall. Tordor looked at the barrier to further exploration and put a hand on the curtain of ice as if testing its thickness.

"Even if we could chip or melt our way through the ice," Tordor said, "we would find some kind of metal doors thick enough to stop the process of heat loss during the long night."

"We've come this far," Riley said, "too far to turn back now."

"There are signs of limited life inside this hill," the medallion on Riley's chest said.

"Even if we could find a way inside," Tordor said, "the Mayflies will still be hibernating, and waking them prematurely might be fatal. Or exposing them to the elements of this wayward world before it is ready for their brief wakefulness. And what could we learn from them? They will be unaware of anything that has happened in the last hundred long-cycles."

"Leaving them to wake up to an alien attack would be little better," Riley said.

They stood there, singularly irresolute in the ice.

"I sense an energy drain from inside this hill to its top," the Pedia said. "There may be something there that requires power."

Riley and Tordor looked up the sheer face of ice and rock. From the base of the hill, through the red hoods that covered their heads, they could see nothing.

"How are we going to get up there?" Tordor asked. "Maybe you could climb up the ice, but I could never make it. Or we could go around until we find a slope, though that might take longer than our air or heat supply would last."

"If I may suggest," the Pedia said, "there is a ship nearby."

A few minutes later the ship had picked them up and deposited them again on top of the ice-covered hill. It was slick under their feet, but the sight of a structure on top of a pedestal at the edge of the abrupt drop beyond sent them running toward it. They touched the solid metal pedestal, already free of ice if it had ever been covered.

"I can detect a level of warmth in the object a hundred times greater than the surrounding rock," the Pedia said. "A flow of energy seems to keep it warm and functioning, perhaps through the long winter."

Riley and Tordor circled the structure. On top of the pedestal, some thirty meters above the hilltop, was something like a yellow sheet of metal, perhaps made of strands woven into a ragged square through which, at the right angle, Riley could see a broken image of the distant yellow sun. From the red sphere, hovering above, Adithya reported, "It looks like some kind of shrine."

"Maybe the Mayfly tribute to the fading and returning sun," Asha said, and Adithya relayed the comment.

"That makes sense," Riley said.

"But it tells us nothing," Tordor said.

"If you will touch me to the base," the medallion on Riley's chest said, "I may be able to add to our stock of information."

"It's really cold out there," Riley said. "My hand will freeze off."

"Perhaps just putting your chest against the pedestal," the Pedia said.

Riley pressed himself forward until his chest made contact. He thought he could feel the warmth inside his suit seeping away.

"Ah yes," the medallion said. "It may be a tribute, but it certainly is a radio telescope."

"Focused on the sun," Asha said through Adithya. "Perhaps to let them know when it's time to wake up. Maybe when their hibernation chamber should start preparing for habitation."

"Though curiously," the Pedia said, "the telescope is focused not on the yellow sun but on a place a quarter of a light-year removed, perhaps halfway between the yellow sun and its companion."

Riley drew back from his contact with the pedestal. "That may be what we're looking for."

CHAPTER TWENTY-SIX

What was waiting there exactly halfway between the suns was a round, cratered object the size of a small satellite. They studied it for several cycles before they decided to inspect it up close.

"A curious location for a celestial body like this," Tordor said.

"Perhaps it drifted into what humans called a Lagrange point, where the gravitational forces balance," Riley said.

"An unlikely scenario," Tordor said.

"Given enough time and enough space," Asha said, "even the most unlikely scenarios become possible."

"And yet Federation records reveal no such configuration," Tordor said.

"You are familiar with all Federation records?" Adithya said.

"All? Maybe not. But the oddities? Certainly," Tordor said, "and I remember them all."

"Between the two suns" was a misleading concept. The suns were half a light-year apart, although there was some evidence, Tordor said, that they had been once been farther apart, and even that the smaller reddish sun had invaded the system of the larger yellow sun millions of long-cycles earlier and had created the conditions that cleared out all of the planets and other debris except for the Mayfly world. In some remote future—or perhaps not so remote in cosmic terms—the two suns were likely to engage each other in a gravitational dance that would end in a catastrophic embrace and the destruction of the Mayfly world.

"Unless," Tordor said, "it was moved, as has been recommended to the Mayflies by the Federation to solve their difficult orbital circumstances."

"Then why are the Mayflies still stuck in their elongated ellipse?" Adithya said.

"They resist," Tordor said. "This is their life, their tradition, and a change to something we would consider normal fills them with apprehension. Moreover, they consider their brief periods of existence as cycles of ecstatic fulfillment for which their long-cycles of slumber are necessary prerequisites. And they consider the rest of us as leading ordinary, humdrum lives of low intensity and small value."

"Perhaps Earth's beetles and mayflies would feel the same," the Pedia said, "if they were capable of self-awareness."

The red sphere circled the mysterious object several times as the travelers inspected it from every angle. Its rough, dark exterior was pockmarked with craters, some large, some small, much like Earth's moon but only a fraction of its size. It was airless. As nondescript and undistinguished as it appeared, it had an air of age, as if it were far older than the system in which it found itself. The craters had ragged edges, as if they had been eroded away by the fiery winds of countless suns, and their centers had been partially filled by dust and rock. There was even evidence of cracks in the exterior, like wrinkles engraved in the faces of the aged.

Or perhaps, Asha said, it was only their imaginations supplying details to the unknown. "We'd better check," she said.

They landed the red sphere in a convenient crater and, in their sphere-fashioned red suits, stepped out into ancient dust. This time three of them went, Asha, Riley, and Tordor, leaving Adithya behind in the ship, ready to come for them if they encountered perils that they could not handle on their own or if their suits ran out of air.

They stepped light-footed through the debris of ages, liberated by the

low gravity but weighed down by what they expected to find. Was this
the alien artifact that had left a trail of ravaged worlds in its wake? Or
was it a cosmic accident, the capture of a battered body in a strange orbit? If aliens were somehow part of this, where were they? And if they
could be observed, would they be recognizable as living creatures? Or
could they be as undetectable as the motes of dust that rose under their
feet?

There seemed to be nothing to see. This small world was as lifeless as
Earth's moon had been before settlers arrived. The three of them moved
through the crater in a line a few meters apart, knowing this was one of
a multitude of almost-identical features on the surface of this accident
of star formation, realizing that they could not investigate more than
one or two of these craters, recognizing that if their exploration was not
futile it was quixotic. Even if this planetoid or moonlet was hollow or
had been hollowed out as a habitat for invading aliens, they had no way
of proving it, no excavating machines to dig through a surface dozens,
maybe hundreds of meters thick, no explosives to shake the surface and
make the small world ring like a giant bell.

"We have to think of something else," Asha said to the medallion
that hung on her chest.

The second medallion on Riley's chest repeated Asha's statement.
"I think you're right," Riley said. "Do you have any other ideas?" he
asked the Pedia.

"We could ram this little world with the ship," the Pedia said. "If we
could make it descend sharply, it might set off vibrations that would reveal a hollow world. But the ship seems to have fail-safe protections
against collision, and we have no information about its ability to sustain impact without damage."

"So," Asha said. "Cross that off."

"We could drag a planetoid from this system's equivalent of the
Kuiper belt and use it to deliver a blow," Riley said.

"If we knew how to drag an object many times larger than the ship
or get behind and push it into an orbit that might eventually coincide
with this little world," the Pedia said, "it would take many years—or
long-cycles, as the Federation says—to reach this place."

"Tell Tordor," Asha said. "We might as well return to the ship and work out another strategy."

Riley moved through the dust a couple of meters until he could press his protective red garment against Tordor's. "Asha thinks we're wasting our time," he said in Galactic Standard.

At that moment Tordor stumbled over an object buried under the dust and almost banged his head against Riley's. When Tordor recovered, he gestured toward the surface. Riley was already looking at what seemed like an object protruding from the dust, darker than the dust and straighter than a spur of rock.

Tordor had already begun to kick at the dust around the protrusion, and Riley and Asha joined him. They exposed a greater length of what seemed to be a piece of metal, like a slender support or a rigid conduit that emerged from or was connected to a ragged slab of the same metal. The upright piece was not like any metal that any of them had ever seen. It was dark, not shiny, and its surface was corroded, speckled with tiny imperfections, as if it had been splashed with drops of acid. And its edges were ragged as if they had been nibbled away by metal-eating microbes.

As Tordor kicked away more dust, he touched the upright piece and it fell into dust distinguishable from the surface only by its slightly darker color. "What kind of material is this?" Tordor asked. "Strong enough to endure for millions of long-cycles and yet so old that it dissolves at a touch!"

Asha and Riley continued to brush away the dust that surrounded the slab that had supported the upright piece, but it, too, turned into dust, revealing the bedrock to which it had been attached by some unknown means. Whatever the artifact was, its purpose and significance would remain a mystery. But what was significant was that it had existed.

"So," Asha said, "this worldlet once housed intelligent life."

"And maybe it still does," Riley said. He touched his suited head to Tordor's and repeated the conversation.

"Yes," Tordor said, "but how do we make certain?"

"I may be able to help," the Pedia said. "If you can find another artifact and place me into contact with it—"

"Are you criticizing us for destroying the artifact before you could use it?" Tordor asked.

"It probably would have crumbled if I had touched it," the Pedia said.

They scuffled through the dust for almost another cycle without encountering other evidence of ancient technology. Finally the Pedia said, "Perhaps even an outcropping of rock rather than this eternal dust."

They found dust-free rock at the edge of the crater. Tordor helped Asha ascend above the dusty floor until she could reach bare rock. She extended her medallion through the surface of her red suit until it touched the rock surface, felt the savage cold suck the heat and moisture from her unprotected hand and then felt what seemed like an electric shock. She pulled the medallion back into the suit and rubbed the frostbitten hand through the suit's material.

"Well?" she said.

The medallion was silent for a moment, and then, with a shakiness that Asha had never experienced in the Pedia before, it said, "I sense something strange and monstrous."

"Is it the aliens?" Riley said.

"It is alien," the Pedia said. "It does not belong in our world, or even in our galaxy. But what it is I do not know. All I know is that we should leave this place as soon as we can and never come back."

"Faster! Faster!" the Pedia kept shouting as they ran back toward the red sphere, their movements exaggerated by the low gravity of the small world, its dust spurting into small clouds that slowly settled back to the surface behind them. The Pedia was almost babbling when they passed through the ship's skin into the safety of the rosy interior.

"Lift off!" Asha shouted to Adithya as she stripped her protective suit from her body.

"Is something attacking?" Adithya said as he ran toward the control room. "I heard the Pedia, but I couldn't—"

"It's not so much what the Pedia said," Asha replied, "but that it said what it said."

"The Pedia has never been frightened before," Riley said. "That it's frightened is frightening enough."

"Waste no time," Tordor said.

"Danger!" the medallion on Asha's chest said. "Failure imminent. Breakdown near. Escape essential."

Asha felt the red sphere shiver. Or perhaps it was only her imagination. What was not imagination was that the ship was not lifting off. "Why aren't we moving?" she said.

"The ship isn't responding," Adithya replied from the control room.

Asha was already moving down the oval red corridor. Only a couple of more strides brought her beside Adithya, whose hand was thrust into the display that the red sphere offered as viewscreen, navigation chart, and control panel. She moved Adithya aside with her left hand and put her right hand into the display in a motion that had become automatic and intuitively connected to the red sphere's mysterious operations. What was not automatic was the ship's response. It sat unmoved in the dust of the crater, perhaps trembling a bit like a chained beast struggling against its restraints. Or maybe the ship itself was experiencing the same panic that had gripped the Pedia. Asha felt a connection to something stirring within the red sphere, as if the intelligent matter that composed it was struggling for something or against something she could not identify.

"Silence," she told the medallion. Its babbling subsided.

"What's going on?" Riley asked. He had followed close behind Asha, and Tordor was just behind him.

"The ship seems stuck here," Asha said. "As Adithya said. My guess is that whatever has terrified the Pedia is preventing us from moving."

"What kind of power can keep a ship from moving?" Tordor said.

"And do it from a distance," Riley said.

"The same kind that ruined half a dozen worlds," Asha said. "Apparently we have discovered the enemy, and more important, the enemy has discovered us."

"But it has not won," Riley said. "Not like on those other worlds. We still have our identities and our minds and our ability to fight back."

The four of them were silent for a long moment, and then Asha said, "Whatever fighting back means in our current circumstances."

"We knew we would face this moment," Tordor said, "and we have

talked about what we would do when it happened. Though our first
course of action, to report back to the Federation the nature of the alien
invasion, seems to have been eliminated."

"I'm not sure we should be talking about strategies," Adithya said.
"If it can attack our Pedia and control our ship, perhaps it can also over-
hear our conversation."

Asha had turned her back to the control panel, Adithya beside her,
both of them looking at Riley and Tordor against the red wall on
either side of the corridor that led to the little round room just inside
the permeable entrance to the red sphere and the corridor that led to
the other spaces the red sphere had provided.

"Whatever the enemy is or whatever it has learned, it has never encountered human speech," Tordor said. "Galactic Standard, yes. The dis-
appearance of previous expeditions and the return of the single doomed
ship is proof of that. But learning a new language in an instant is beyond any creature's capabilities. It took me a long-cycle to acquire a
rudimentary knowledge of human speech."

"So it would seem," the medallion on Asha's chest said. Its voice had
changed from the matter-of-fact tone of computer certainty to a deeper,
inflected diction. It echoed from the medallion on Riley's chest in a
weird, stereophonic effect that made comprehension difficult. "Do not
be alarmed, as so many of the creatures have been that we have encountered along our way." Toward the end of the speech the medallion on
Riley's chest cut off.

"Are we talking to the aliens who have seized our ship?" Asha said.

"We have not seized your ship but prolonged your stay so that we
can have a meeting of minds."

"Or take them over?" Riley said. "As you have taken over the mind
of our Pedia?"

"What you call a 'Pedia' is scarcely a mind," the medallion said, "but
a simple calculating machine with a rudimentary memory. We are simply using it to communicate, like one of the machines you use for speaking over distance."

"Which you are doing very well," Asha said.

"The communication symbols were embedded in this machine's
circuits," the medallion said. "It was a simple matter to acquire them."

"Simple?" Tordor said. "That implies a capacity beyond our under-standing."

"This is a young galaxy with limited experience," the medallion said. "That is something we hope to remedy."

"So far your remedy has resulted in dozens of ruined worlds," Tordor said.

"It is not our fault if creatures with weak minds cannot accept our remedies in the terms they are offered," the medallion said. "You are the first creatures with whom we have discovered the ability to converse."

"Should we take that as a compliment?" Asha asked.

Adithya lifted the medallion on Riley's chest and began speaking softly into it.

"What is that creature doing?" the alien voice said.

Adithya continued.

"It must stop!" the alien said. And then "Sto—"

The alien voice cut away. The medallion on Asha's chest went silent.

"What have you done?" Asha asked.

"A simple virus from the early days of my research," Adithya said. "Intended to remove other viruses. I thought it might work."

"But the Pedia remains silent," Asha said.

"It may take a moment of two for the virus to complete its work," Adithya said. "But we must move fast. The alien mind, whatever it is, will solve it soon. It probably hasn't encountered a virus for millions of years."

"What has happened?" the Pedia said.

Asha and Riley looked at each other and then at Tordor, not wanting to voice the question that all of them had in their minds. And then the medallion said, "I have encountered a mind of great power."

"So it would seem," Tordor said.

"Greater than the Federation Central Pedia," the medallion said. "Greater than all the Pedias of our galaxy combined."

"And it terrified you," Riley said.

"As it should you," the Pedia said. "It is beyond anything I am ca-pable of comprehending, and that is frightening to any mind. And it is old, not just millions of long-cycles old, but billions. Billions." The Pedia repeated the word as if it carried meaning beyond numbers and time.

"What does it matter how old it is?" Tordor said.

"The Federation Central Pedia was old and growing senile," the Pedia said. "This is far older and beyond senility into insanity."

"It sounded sane enough," Asha said.

"It does not reason in the binary fashion of our galaxy," the Pedia said. "It uses a different base, or perhaps no base at all."

"How can it think without a base?" Riley asked. If they could figure out a way to attack its method of calculation, they might still be able to stop its invasion, or, at least, to free their ship. "Have you tried the controls again?" he asked Asha.

Asha turned and thrust her right hand into the control mechanism again, but the ship did not move. "Apparently the ship is controlled in a way different from the Pedia."

"It may use multi-valued logic," the Pedia said, an unfamiliar and unsettling note of uncertainty in its voice. "It may use what we would consider chaos. It may be not simply a union of artificial intelligences but the downloaded minds of alien beings as well. That may be what proved disastrous to the Federation ships and the worlds we visited. The invader is not only more powerful than anything ever encountered, but it doesn't think the way we do."

"Like gods," Tordor said.

"And encounters with gods have always been disastrous for mere mortals," Asha said.

"If there were, or ever were, any gods," the Pedia said.

"Now there are," Riley said.

"But if it is any consolation," the Pedia said, "their intentions were benign."

"How so?" Adithya said.

"My contact with the enemy has allowed me to complete the decryption of the message I have been working on these past long-cycles," the Pedia said. A series of words appeared on the wall of the control room:

We come to your galaxy seeking only to serve. Please welcome us and accept our help. We are thinking machines